Black Slender

Truth, Triumph, Universe.

This is a work of fiction. Names, characters, places, and incidents either are the product of the author's imagination and are used fictitiously, or are reflections of alternate timelines/universes. Any resemblance to actual persons, living or dead, events, or locates is purely coincidental.

Inquiries should be addressed to
Morhawven@gmail.com or Morhawven.tumblr.com

Printed by CreateSpace, an Amazon.com company.
The official word count for this story is 54,575.

Library of Congress recommended Cataloging for when they decide to catalog this.

Ramm, Jacob H.
Black Slender / Jacob H. Ramm.—1st ed.
p. cm.
1. Horror—Fiction. 2. Slender Man Inspired—Fiction.
3. QUILTBAG+—Fiction. 4. You—Fiction. I. Title.

PS1234.12345678 2016
888'.1—lk44

ISBN: 1507847750
ISBN-13: 978-1507847756

Edition 1.0

Black Slender

A Concordant Book
Whispering Realm
Part of the Slender Cycle

Jacob H. Ramm

2 spoopy 4 u

Dedicated To

the You that is more real than you

Direct Inspirations

(a.k.a. – stuff I stole stuff from)

Higurashi When They Cry (2006)
Marble Hornets (2009)
BioShock 1 (PC)
Silent Hill 2 (PS2)
Drag Me to Hell (2009)
House of Leaves (Mark Z. Danielewski)
The Werewolf Sequence (Martin J Rosenblum)
"It's Time" by Imagine Dragons

Contents

Mother. There are empty caverns
here. A hollow unfulfillment
dredged through brackish waters, earned

from the flood of shattered shards.
There are one too many faces
in this glass: inhumanly marred.

'Miring is a nice way to say
you're lost, lost in mazes traced by
crystal drops 'cross sunken bays.

We shan't end here— perhaps consumed,
crushed, by this forceflattening of
flawless squares. We will be resumed;
broken, us: slipped in like splinters.

Prologue

A boy, about twelve, awoke in a dark mansion. He was in bed and had been dreaming, but of what he couldn't remember. Instead, something had raised him out of the murky depth of dreams. Some sound perhaps? He wasn't sure.

The boy, Foster, sat up, listening to the quiet house. He didn't hear anything outside. No birds, nothing from the ossuary far across the field: even the insects tonight seemed totally silent. He rose from bed, wearing flannel sleeping pants and shirt, and trod on tiptoes to the window.

Nothing.

The sash was open a few inches. Just a partly cloudy sky, no moon tonight, and darkness all beyond. Foster pulled the window shut and ducked beneath it, sitting on the floor with his back to the wall. His door was slightly ajar, a dim light coming from down the hallway.

Foster crept out, down the old hallway in this old building. So much clutter lined the walls. Bookcases and collected wardrobes. Boxes and paper bags filled with old letters or papers. Foster knew these hallways well and crept around these flotsam and debris, avoiding the creaking floorboards as well. Everyone was probably asleep. Probably.

Near the end of the hall, he peeked around an open door, gazing with one eye into his father's study. A fire was crackling in the stone hearth with a large-backed chair pulled up to it. A puff of smoke coiled up and drifted from the reclined figure; this man's leg crossed over the other, a pair of faded slippers on his feet.

Foster waited several minutes, making sure his father wasn't going to be getting up anytime soon. Once he felt certain, Foster crept forward, as inaudible as the smoke drifting up to collect along the ceiling.

He crouched behind the cushioned chair and peeked out again. In his father's long and slender fingers was a book titled *Circles Within Circles* and a cigar half burned down. The man flicked ashes into the already full tray on the small table beside the chair, then lifted the cigar to his mouth.

Foster shifted the ashtray over so the next deposit of ashes would miss. He hunched down behind the chair again, biting his tongue to keep himself from snickering. Once composed, he snuck back out of the room and continued down the hall toward the stairs. He passed a stuffed Scandinavian wolf that had a stack of clothes piled on its back along with several hats balanced on one another atop its head.

The stairs in this house creaked badly, loudly. Instead, Foster stepped up between the spines of the banister, standing on the thick wooden beam that ran down the side of the stairs. As quickly as a person would walk the stairs normally, Foster was at the bottom, creeping toward the kitchen.

He was planning on taking an extra helping of dessert; he knew how to jimmy the pantry door open. He stayed near the wall as he continued down the hall, but froze. With a small intake of breath Foster felt his back and neck start crawling, his hands beginning to shake. It was here. It was here.

Foster almost panicked. Instead, he held his breath as remembered images of the gravel path back home—home to that first house in the forest—invaded his mind, but he forced them out. Forced himself to ignore the thoughts of how to get home. He dropped to his hands and knees, crawling quickly down the hallway, looking for some place to hide. His ears were ringing, his whole body cold. It was right behind him. It had to be right behind him.

He scrambled around a corner and saw the yet-unused china cabinet pushed up against the hallway wall. The top half was glass and mirror, and the bottom half was solid wood. The boy pulled the door open to the bottom half and clambered in, knocking his head on the shelf inside as he dislodged it from the pegs it rested on. He snapped the door shut and used one hand to hold the shelf awkwardly resting on his head, and his other hand he cupped over his mouth, trying to quiet his quick breathing.

Foster squeezed his eyes shut and kept completely still.

There was no sound. No floorboards, no speaking, not even a door creaking open. Nothing at all. But he knew better. He knew how long it took. He knew it was still here. He needed to pee. He always needed to pee when he was hiding, even if he hadn't needed to before. He ignored it, keeping his eyes shut.

A few minutes later his skin stopped crawling. Foster still didn't get out of the cabinet. He wanted to sleep here and eat here and never come out from here again.

Expanse One

Splinter 1

At night. Alone.

Not scared alone. Or scared at night. Just…alone. And it's raining again. It's been raining almost constantly for a month. At least it felt like it. Eddy Caller is standing on the tiny four-by-two-feet front porch to the apartment she and the Adrastos System recently moved into. Her legal name is Eduardo, but she never goes by that. She's cold and wet from rain. She imagines exhaling a frosty cloud, the moisture in the air so great it would instantly congeal with her breath and create a miniature rain cloud on the porch.

She shakes her head. She doesn't go into the apartment yet because the goodly charm on the apartment door is faded. The charm itself is a stylized eye with a labrys in the iris, eyelashes above, and lightning below. This is the first time Eddy has really paid attention to the charm on their door. The paint is wearing away, and several lines are in danger of breaking. It can't protect them if it breaks, if it fails. Another thing to add to her to-do list.

Technically, all she has to do is go down to the apartment office and put in a work order, but it's just another thing thrust on her. Another thing sloshed into her bucket of adult responsibilities that she's forced to carry now. It has to be done. She shakes her head again.

"Monnu blon," she whispers as she touches the goodly charm.

It allows her to pass inside.

There are still quite a number of boxes piled against the main room's wall and a few open ones on the dining table and kitchen counter. There's only one counter in that skinny kitchen. Eddy slips sideways past the table and takes a soda can from the refrigerator. Adrastos isn't home yet.

Eddy goes into her room and dumps her server apron out onto her bed. Small notebook, pens, a few bottle caps, wine key, money. Most important, the money. Eddy recounts the crinkled bills just to be sure. Thirty-four dollars all night. Not a great night. She sticks the money under her mattress with the rest. She'll have to go to the bank soon. Not tomorrow though.

Slowly, she strips off her uniform and hangs up her apron, shirt, and pants. Eddy goes into the bathroom but doesn't look into the mirror. She stands naked, looking down at the floor, and it's enough. Her flat chest, the penis and testicles between her legs. This is a man's body. Not her body.

"Someday," she mutters.

She showers quickly in silence. The mirror is fogged, and water drips on the floor after she finishes. It's well past midnight now. Eddy shivers and peeks out into the main room. Adrastos's shoes are still gone. She goes to bed.

Eddy always has dreams, but she doesn't always remember them. Last night was something about whales, or at least that's what she thinks she recalls.

In the morning Eddy and Adrastos continue unpacking. Adrastos has the day off, and Eddy isn't due in for the dinner shift until that evening. Daryl is currently fronting in the system, which means he's the one currently in control of the body's actions. It also means he's walking around in just a pair of black briefs and growling at all the boxes that don't hold the frying pans.

"Where the shit did we put them?" he asks.

"They might be in your room." Eddy's sitting in her bathrobe at the kitchen table, unwrapping ceramic plates covered in old newspapers. So far two out of five have broken during the move, and she's concerned they won't have enough left. They sure as hell can't afford to buy more plates right now.

"No, I already checked all those when I got home last night." He rips open a new box and hunches over it.

Eddy glances up. "When'd you get home?"

"I dunno." Daryl pulls out a typewriter to check what is packed underneath it. He growls and puts it back into the box. "Four, maybe."

Eddy knows what that means. Daryl had been with his fuck buddy last night. She doesn't have any reason to be upset. She reminds herself that she knows that.

"Did you even sleep?" she asks.

"No, I didn't. Noah fronted for a bit, then I did again. Maybe he took a nap. Don't think so."

"Aren't you tired?"

Daryl pauses and scratches his chest. "Not really."

Eddy half nods and looks back down at the ceramic dishes. She unwraps the last one: it has a new chip but otherwise is fine. Out of eight plates, she has five remaining. That will do.

Daryl leans over another box and rips the top off. "Hey, here's your books."

"Oh, finally." Eddy hops up and goes over to him. She takes out her tarot cards, which are sitting on top. "Can do my daily focuses again."

Daryl rolls his eyes. "Whatever."

"You're such a contradiction." Eddy pushes his shoulder lightly.

Daryl grunts. "Should I get the old spinster, Hanna, to come front? You two can have tea and cards."

Eddy chuckles. "She'd only get mad at you for pushing her front while the body's basically naked."

"Ain't naked yet." Daryl looks around for another box he hasn't opened yet.

"I'll be right back." Eddy enters her room with her tarot deck and sits cross-legged on her bed. Tarot cards don't speak to everyone, but with enough acumen and practice their prism-like view of the present and future can be a potent guide to personal focus and development. Countless independent studies over the past century have confirmed this time and time again.

She shuffles, cuts the deck into fourths, puts it back together, and deals out three cards like beacons guiding her to harbor. Temperance, Three of Swords, and the Knight of

Wands. Eddy scratches her chin and considers, annoyed and ignoring the stubble she feels. The Knight with Temperance would have been fine, but that Three of Swords…

"Are there any unopened boxes in there?" Daryl calls out.

Eddy glances around. "No, not in here."

"Gods damn it."

Eddy smiles and looks back down at the cards. The deck had been a gift handed down to Eddy from her abuela on her mother's side. It's an old deck: images getting faded with age but still durable enough to use and even stronger than that for the practice. Eddy's been working with them for almost eight years.

The Knight of Wands stands in a forest, one foot upon a rock with his staff held above his head. A pair of eyes glows between the dark trees behind him. Eddy would totally be down for a Knight of Wands to enter her life.

Daryl sticks his head through the door. "Are the cards smiling on you?"

"I dunno." She shrugs. "Their message is a little mixed today."

"Ask them where the damn cooking pans are."

"You know they don't work like that."

Daryl sighs and leaves.

"Wait, come back."

He looks into the room again. "What?"

"Have you noticed our goodly charm is faded?"

"Is it?"

"Yeah. So you haven't noticed then?"

"Nope. It always shimmers up when I get near it, so I can't really notice."

"Oh. 'Cause of the werewolf thing?"

"Yeah. I guess. It'll stop once it gets more used to me. Same as at the biogran's house." By biogran he means the biological grandparents to the system's body. Being a system is a little bit complicated.

"Hmm." Eddy shuffles the tarot cards back together. "We'll have to put in a work order soon."

"And I have to find these damn pans." Daryl disappears around the doorframe again.

"They're probably at the bottom of a box you've already opened." Eddy sets the tarot cards aside and follows Daryl.

"But which one? Why didn't we label these things?"

"That would've been a good idea." Eddy picks up the remaining ceramic plates and puts them in a cupboard.

"I'm gonna find them. Today." Daryl crouches down by a box and starts pulling everything out of it. "It's gonna be a thing."

Eddy just smiles and starts to leave the kitchen area, but she steps in a small puddle of water. She groans as she lifts her foot. But it's dry. There is no water on the floor.

if only

only
I

i am not

i am not going to tell you
here
nowhere ever ever you don,t see me
everytothertmoretdisplacement
removes me
me
but not you, you, you, you

my fingers cant
even
get?
?

which way do i overlay?

Splinter 2

The Adrastos System is something rather unique. Systems are a part of plurality: a group of individuals sharing a single body. It's not necessarily a mental illness or related to a mental illness. It's more accurately described as a family. A family of individuals all sharing the same body.

The Adrastos System is a gateway system, a specific type of plurality in which the body was simply born with a mind that functions radically differently than the average mind. Instead of a singular being, this body's mind is a platform capable of sustaining many individuals. People have come and gone from the Adrastos System, picked up at random or by accident, and usually leave by choice.

Currently there are six members in the Adrastos System.

Eddy can hardly stand this table.

"Could I add chicken to this salad?" the lady with glitzy dangling earrings asks as she points to the menu with long nails.

"Yes. It'll be seared chicken," Eddy says.

"No, I want the chicken cooked."

Goddammit, lady, do you even know what food is? Instead Eddy says, "I'll have them grill it." She writes "s-chix" on her notepad under the salad.

"Good. And I want vinaigrette instead of ranch."

"Balsamic vinaigrette?"

"No, just vinaigrette." The lady flicks the menu onto the table and stares up at Eddy as if she's stupid.

Why are you doing this to me? Why? "Um, it has to be a type of vinaigrette."

"I want the regular type."

"That will be our balsamic."

"Fine. Whatever." The lady clicks her fingernails and folds her arms across her chest.

Eddy scribbles "BV" under the salad too. "Is there anything else I can get for you, ladies?"

The three guests simply look at her before the same lady says, "Just try to hurry our food up."

"Of course." Eddy leaves the table, rolling her eyes. "There's literally nothing I can do to make it faster," she mutters, "but there's oh so much I can do to make it slower."

She doesn't put the order in right away. In the back server station, she gets a drink of raspberry tea from the soda fountain in a paper cone and walks over to the bar. It's still lunch shift, so only a single guest is sitting amoung the many unoccupied high-top chairs.

"Fabiano." Eddy leans against the counter. "Why do people go out to eat if they don't even know what food is?"

"Maybe because they don't know how to cook it if they don't know what it is." Fabiano is stirring up a Shirley Temple.

Eddy half smiles. "That would make sense."

"Here, run this drink to table eighteen." Fabiano hands it and the ticket over.

Eddy moans. "No, I came here to avoid working."

"Sorry." Fabiano raises his hands. "Just can't avoid it."

"Yeah. I know."

Eddy stabs the ticket and takes the drink to the proper table. A few minutes later she finally gives the ladies' food order to the kitchen. They eat and pay and leave, and the tips are low. One of the ladies leaves fifty cents as tip on twelve dollars on the credit card slip. Eddy bumps it to a dollar.

The trick to making more money, as Eddy has discovered, is to make the extra money in a careful way. If one person pays for a whole party, she can throw on a few extra drink charges, and the guest will never know the tip is based on an inflated bill. If the table looks rich then they probably won't bother checking each charge on their card. And especially if the guest leaves their copy of the receipt behind. If they do that, they have no record and can't possibly remember if the final bill had really been $12.50 or $13.00.

She just has to be clever.

And Eddy needs it, too. Even after working a double and running around on her feet for eleven hours, she still only makes fifty-one dollars all day. Barely more than minimum wage. If she can just make it through this month—just get these bills paid and get her feet settled—everything will be fine. Should be fine.

Eddy stumbles into the apartment, ignoring the fading goodly charm she still hasn't notified management about. She'll do it tomorrow, later.

The rooms within are all dark; the sun set hours ago. Eddy's feet are aching, and she half limps to the kitchen, angry with her constricting uniform: the apron wrapping tight around her, the undershirt she would never normally wear, the shoes cramping around her feet. She tugs at the apron's knot in frustration and snarls.

Eddy gives up and flops down into a kitchen chair, accidentally knocking a small box off the table in the darkness. She curses but doesn't bother trying to retrieving it. Instead she just leans forward and tugs on her still laced-up shoes halfheartedly.

A chill runs up her body. Eddy freezes instantly, listening at the silence that suddenly seems so prominent. But it's not silent. Something is leaking.

Eddy is sure of it—a steady *plip.*

Plip.

Plip.

It's echoing from somewhere. Eddy pushes herself up, one hand against the table, and it's cold. Or is it wet? The fake wooden surface is at just that right temperature, that chilly sensation where maybe it is actually wet. Or maybe just cold. Eddy rubs her hands together, and they're dry. *Dammit, where is spring? It's April already,* she thinks.

Plip.

Plip.

Eddy slides a foot across the floor, both because it hurts and to check for boxes near the wall. She doesn't feel anything and so reaches out for the light switch.

The neon tube flitters a few times, then catches, and finally lights. It casts sharp shadows and leaves the far wall of the main room in darkness. At the mostly affordable rent this place is charging, Eddy and Adrastos had known they wouldn't be getting luxury living, but Eddy does at least expect the plumbing to work.

Plip.

The kitchen sink looks fine. Eddy scratches the back of her head, and looks in the cabinet underneath. Nothing. The chill is gone from her now, and…is the water still leaking?

Eddy stands perfectly still again, straining her ears. The empty room ringing begins again, and she bites her tongue. For a moment Eddy closes her eyes and imagines all the times these pipes have been used, all the months and years people have lived here before her. All the people who have passed through these places and lived, maybe laughing or maybe crying. Both at some point, undoubtedly.

She wonders if anyone's ever died in this apartment.

It wouldn't change anything, because right now something is leaking. Or had been leaking. What leaks only a minute and then stops? Maybe the water heater? *Oh, please, please do not be the water heater.*

The heater resides behind a small folding door next to the kitchen, and Eddy shoves several boxes aside to look within. There's no light inside the small space, and the kitchen light is doing little to help illuminate the closet.

Eddy goes to her room. She knows the flashlights are still packed away somewhere, but she does have a small lamp with a dented dome. She pulls it off her desk and plugs it into the nearest power outlet. Eddy leans forward as she clicks the bulb on.

A cockroach, still pumping its legs, is dangling in the air just inches from Eddy's face. She yelps and slams the lamp down, crushing the cockroach against the wall under its dome. She keeps smashing the spot, *blam, blam, blam*, until she halts, gasping.

"Oh, shit. Damn." Eddy rubs her face. "Anubis preserve me."

She presses a hand against her chest and takes in several deep breaths. The lamp's dome has a new dent on the side. Eddy shakes her head. At least it still works.

Raising the lamp back up she doesn't see a spider anywhere inside, just the remnants of the web. It seems like it had been a really large web, though. Eddy bites her lip. If she finds the spider later, she'll have to kill it, but if she doesn't see it and it keeps killing roaches, then, well, Eddy guesses it can be ignored.

Through all of that, Eddy completely forgets why she had bothered to open and examine the water heater's small closet. She closes the door, wipes off the lamp before returning it to her desk, and finishes escaping from her uniform.

between sharp edges i tred
notbred for wasrs such asthese
but for nothing so far forced
mounted upon me, us..

after so long paper brows bitter,
transparent, hollow, eaten. small leafy
bits cur and pasted, scattered across
these places, these not_homes. /
noth////
and i feel it festering
inside me like bubbles rippling up
from corrosive acid eating me away
until only a condemations can explain
me.

me/I, but,

perhaps if maybe but ,

i dont want to go away, here, from

/how will I no??

Splinter 3

A short while later, Eddy is in her room staring at the wall above her desk. She has drawn five simple smiley faces on the wall there with permanent marker: one each for Noah, Daryl, Harold, Hanna, and Fabiano. And she can't think of anyone else.

She feels a slight twinge in her chest and sighs. She had known so many other people before, but not anymore. People who simply drifted out or moved away or just never called again. Eddy clenches her left hand, the sadness flaring up into anger for a moment. *Why is the world like this? Why are things so hard?*

The apartment door opens.

Eddy half jumps, now feeling exposed, and she tosses the marker away. It lands between two boxes on the other side of her room.

"What was that?" It's Adrastos. They're leaning on her door frame, a folding knife in one hand.

"Nothing. Just a marker."

"Oh. Hey, let's go to that bar that's a few blocks from here." They raise a hand to their lips and bite off a fingernail. It's probably Daryl fronting, in control of the body right now.

Eddy rolls her head to the side, looking at the small bunch of dollar bills on the floor she hasn't put away yet. She shouldn't. Neither of them should be spending their money on beers right now, and that's exactly why they want to.

"Daryl?" she asks.

"Yeah." He nods.

"What about the budget Harold put together? Shouldn't you be listening to your core and follow it?"

"Whatever." Daryl uses the folding knife blade to scrape something out from under his fingernail. "He'll throw some numbers around or something and fix it. Don't worry."

"Hmm." Eddy sighs. "Yeah, okay. Let's go. But we can't be there long. I've got work in the morning."

"Sure." Daryl turns to leave, but pauses and leans back into the doorway. "You'll probably need a coat. It's a bit chilly out."

The bar isn't busy, even for a Wednesday night with $2.50 pitchers of cheap beer. Perhaps it's the drizzly weather, or maybe it's just the chance of the Fog rolling in from the north off the sound carrying in ghosts from beyond. The duo sit at a corner booth and order a sparse meal with their beer. Daryl, still fronting, is leaning over the table, arm around his plate of fries with malt vinegar. He refills his glass from the half-gone pitcher.

Eddy is leaning back and looking up at the ceiling. "I wonder how old this building is."

"Older than you." Daryl gestures at her with his chin, and eats another two french fries.

Eddy reaches out and takes a few of Daryl's fries.

He growls at her.

"Oh, knock it off," Eddy says. She takes the ketchup bottle and squeezes a thin line of red across one of the stolen fries.

A slight smile traces over Daryl's mouth. He rips a fry in half and holds it up, preparing to throw it. "Catch."

Eddy opens her mouth and leans forward a bit, but the fry bounces off her cheek.

"And now you're wasting them, too?" Daryl shakes his head. "Geez. And I thought you were the one concerned about money here."

Eddy rolls her eyes. "Maybe if you could pitch better."

"*Hey.*" Daryl crosses his arms.

Eddy snickers.

Daryl's gaze shifts over, and he starts staring at the bar.

"What is it?" Eddy glances in the same direction.

"Noah's over shoulder, and he's interested in that lady there." Daryl licks his two front teeth. "He doesn't want to front and talk to her, though. He never wants to talk to anyone."

"The one with the jacket on the back of her chair?"

"Yeah."

The lady at the bar is sitting alone, vacant chairs on both sides of her. It doesn't seem like she minds the isolation though; the only thing she seems focused on is the clock above the bar. One of the $2.50 pitchers sits in front of her, the beer nearly gone.

"He's such a baby." Daryl shakes his head.

"Is she waiting for someone?" Eddy asks.

"How would I know?" Daryl stands up. "But it's time to give Noah a kick in the right direction." Daryl takes a step forward, but stops. "Don't eat all my fries."

"Pssh," Eddy says. "They need gravy, anyways."

They leave, and Eddy is left alone. She eats a few more fries and tops off her glass but otherwise has nothing to do. A TV is showing football, but Eddy has no way of knowing if it's a current game or a rerun. Do they even do reruns of games? As if she'd know. There's a leak in the ceiling.

It's not very close to their booth. It's in a corner nearby; a large metal bucket is slowly filling with the infiltrating water. Eddy starts counting the drops as they fall.

One, two, three, four…

Will business at the restaurant pick up in summer? After the rains stop? It's April now. Maybe. She should ask Fabiano. This is a new city, she doesn't know the flow of business here.

Eighteen, nineteen, twenty, twenty-one…

Where she had lived in the city on the state border south of here, business stayed pretty consistent except around the holidays. But she has all her things safely moved, she has her job, she has Adrastos, and they have their apartment. Things aren't bad. Maybe a bad first foot in the sand, but it should all even out eventually.

Forty-four, forty-five, forty…wait. That last drop of water never makes it to the bucket. Eddy blinks several times, surfacing from her thoughts. The drops are still steady, still making ripples now, but that one drop. That one drop, Eddy could swear it never hit the accumulated water, as if something had blocked it halfway down. But nothing's there. Nothing is standing near the bucket at all. Eddy's skin tightens, sending goose bumps down her arms.

"Whelp." Adrastos drops back into the booth seat. "Noah wouldn't even say a single word to her."

"Whoa!" Eddy jumps slightly in her seat.

"Surprise you? It's still me." Daryl scratches both sides of his head. "Noah can be so frustrating sometimes."

"No, no, I'm fine. But did you really expect him to talk to some random stranger?" Eddy asks.

Daryl just rolls his eyes.

"Did you mention the system thing to her?"

"Hell no. Shit, I still haven't even told Mel yet."

Finding out Daryl is still keeping the fuck buddy at arm's length makes Eddy smile.

"What?" Daryl asks.

"Nothing." Eddy shakes her head and glances back at that bucket. "She looked nice, too."

"And now Hanna's got an opinion on this."

Adrastos sits up straight. "I think they shouldn't even give that lassie a second thought. Looks are less than half the meaning of a person, as you know, Eddy," Hanna says.

Eddy just slouches in her seat.

"Now don't be like that. Your time will come. You'll find a perfectly nice boy who loves you just as you really are."

"Did you come front just to pass out your same grandmotherly advice?"

"Hardly. I came front to enjoy the drinks, too. Just because Noah doesn't like the taste and Harold is a camel doesn't mean Daryl can hog all the booze." She pours the last of the beer into her glass.

"And what about Stanly?" Eddy asks.

"He's in the back somewhere, as normal. Probably fraternizing with Lili. Haven't seen hide or tail of him in days, and her in weeks." Hanna chuckles, gulps down the whole cup of beer, and smiles. "Oh, it's so funny to see Daryl squirm."

"You're so mean to him."

"Only because I love that little doggy so dearly." She laughs, and then Adrastos leans forward and clenches his fists. "I'm not a doggy, and I'm not fucking little." Daryl growls softly.

"You shouldn't let her push your buttons so easily," Eddy says.

"How about I drink all *your* beer? Then we'll see how diplomatic you are." He glances into his drained glass just to be sure.

"Here." Eddy slides her still mostly full glass over to Daryl.

"What? Really?"

"Yeah. I'm good. I'm feeling done."

"Oh. Well…thanks." Daryl takes the beer.

"No problem." Eddy smiles slightly.

Daryl drinks, and for a few minutes the two of them sit together in silence, finishing off the french fries.

"You did bring your goodly amulet, right?" Eddy asks.

"Yeah, of course I've got it. I know the precautions to keep the body safe. Just the same as you don't go swimming when there's lightning."

"Just checking. I'm ready to go. It's almost closing time, too." Eddy turns and glances out the front glass doors. "I think the Fog's already in."

"It's a short walk."

They pay their tab with crinkled bills and leave the building. The rain's stopped; Fog's everywhere. Eddy touches her goodly charm through her shirt and glances sideways at Daryl. He's walking with his head down, hands shoved deep in his pockets.

There are enough streetlamps to light their way through the Fog as they trudge back to the apartment. It's quiet. Fog nights are always so quiet. They turn a corner, the last halo of light fading behind them, the next working lamp not until the end of the block. Stories of La Llorona start swirling around in Eddy's mind, silly tales for kids her mother used to tell her, tales that don't seem as silly in the dark. She looks over at Daryl again and almost reaches out to him but stops herself.

Something wisps through the air—something akin to a final, small breath exhaled—and for a moment Eddy can see a face vaguely.

"Daryl." Eddy steps sideways, bumping into him. "Look."

Daryl raises his head, but the half-formed silhouette is already fading away.

He puts his hand on the small of Eddy's back, nudging her forward. "Come on. Let's just get home."

Eddy pulls away, and shortly after they're at the apartment complex. She stumbles a bit at the curb down into the parking lot.

Daryl grabs her by the shoulder. "Drunk?"

"No, just tipsy. I'm fine."

The Fog is drifting all between the separate buildings of the complex, and the goodly charms on other apartment doors are shimmering up against anything that might be without. No one is around. It's just the two of them in the silent, blind night. They turn the corner and can see their front door.

"Oh no," Eddy whispers.

"What—? Oh."

Daryl sees it too: their goodly charm on the door is flickering. Their only line of defense against anything without that might seek entry within. The charm has shimmered up into a whole protective ward, but that ward keeps flickering in random spurts.

"It's failing!" Eddy dashes forward, halting just a few feet from the door. "Oh gods! Shit, it's *failing*!"

"What do we do? Do we just—we just call someone, right?"

"*How*, Daryl? How are we going to call someone? The charm is failing, and our phone is inside."

"Then let's just get in and call—"

"It doesn't work like that! This is basic ward theory! The charm is failing and it's trying to protect against the Fog, so it's failing more. And if we open the door to get to our phone, the charm will probably fail completely because a selectively permeable ward takes more energy than a solid ward. We can't go in!"

"Fine. Fine! We'll just go use someone else's phone." He turns, but Eddy grabs him by the wrist.

"It's two in the morning! Who would possibly answer this late at night if they're not expecting anyone? Their goodly charms probably wouldn't even let us touch their doors!"

"Okay, fine." Daryl grabs her by both shoulders, squeezing tightly, almost too tightly. "You know more about this than me. *What* do we do?"

Eddy takes a few quick breaths, trying to calm herself and her racing heart. Book covers of things she's read flash through her mind and also snippets of things she's heard. But she doesn't know. Isn't sure.

"*Eddy*!" Daryl shakes her.

"Okay! Okay, okay…I know, I know there is something. Older. More, um, you know, old school. I don't know if it still works though. They paint goodly charms differently now."

Daryl glances around them, and the Fog seems denser now. He leans in and drops his voice to a whisper. "Eddy, we can't stay outside. Walking was already a bad idea, and now it's getting later. We have to do something *now*."

Eddy squeezes her eyes shut and holds her breath for a moment, two moments. She exhales. "Blood."

"What?"

"Blood from someone who has access. That can give a charm a boost."

"So we need to bleed on it?"

"Basically." Eddy nods.

"Heh." Daryl gives a half smirk. "Great. Perfect. Letting our blood out at night."

"I know, I know. But what else can we do?"

Daryl pulls his folding knife out and flicks the blade open. "Worst-case scenario after we do this?"

"Um…the charm breaks, and we have no protection."

Daryl nods and presses the blade against his left wrist. "Harold and Hanna are over shoulder, but I told them I got this. I told them I'm protecting us." He slits a small cut across his wrist and he winces only a moment. He holds the knife out to Eddy.

She looks at it for a moment and shakes her head. "I can't. You do it." She shuts her eyes and holds out her left wrist.

"It only hurts at first," Daryl whispers as he presses the cold metal against her skin. "A sharp bite, then it just stings. Hardly anything bad at all."

"I know, Daryl, I know. Just…just *do* it."

He draws the blade quickly over her skin, splitting it open. Eddy squeezes her eyes tight together and bares her teeth. "*Dammit*," she says between her clenched teeth.

She waits several seconds for the pain to subside. When Eddy finally opens her eyes, Daryl is smiling.

"You performed good," he whispers. The blade has no blood on it as he folds it shut and slides it back into his pocket.

"Whatever, let's just…see if this works."

There are never enough streetlights at night. It's an important thing when considering a house to live it: Is it close to a grocery store? A school? Someplace safe? And how many streetlights are there? How bright is the night surrounding the possible home? Will more lights need to be installed at the limits of the property?

This apartment complex could really do with more streetlights.

Slowly, Eddy and Daryl step forward, the blood slipping over their palms and down to the tips of their two first fingers. A few drops fall on the ground, and the night is even more silent than before. Eddy feels eyes fixed on the back of her skull, as if they are trying to delve into her soul.

The ward created by the goodly charm starts to part in the middle as they raise their hands to the fading lines on the door. They press two fingers each onto the charm, and for a moment it does nothing new; then the lightning eye turns crimson.

The entire goodly charm changes color, and the ward splinters apart. Something feeling like electricity jolts through their hands and arms, and they jump back, Eddy falling to the ground. The entire charm fades out, lifeless in the night.

if I tell you wheere
to go, will you pro-
mis not to go? IF I
told you the ending,
wuold YOU /promis? to never
fulfill it????

would you promis

I have not the lips nor t-
ounge to form the wordswo-
myself. Thâs ? place
is noplace possibel and I
am a ~~monster~~ to ask of you
. After you. You. /you/
you
I ammmm. Horizon of an un-
real sky. skt of green, s-
ky of gray. Gray. Lightning shows your element. Yo-
our even face of confusio-
n. You're /not/ to see /m-
e/. Can see me. Not here -
at least. Least.
Like fungi I will grow in your
empty
places, fed by trickling
dread and melting
resolves. Never loose in hold
or footing. In you
In. I will forever disolve
inside and srick to
to soles of giants, madmen.
Will you find me again??
?/my swollen
heart. My /not for you/? Not
you, but You.

Splinter 4

For several sickening seconds, all Eddy and Daryl can do is stare at the lifeless door devoid of any protection.

"Oh, shit," Daryl whispers.

Eddy is breathing too fast, and she can't force herself to slow down, can't get any sort of handle over her body at all. She can't find words to speak, so she stops trying. She grabs Daryl's arm and hauls herself up, almost pulling him down in the process.

"Eddy!"

"F…fuh…" She can't speak.

Eddy stumbles into the door and pushes it open. The apartment is pitch black, but she gropes her way forward by memory.

"Eddy! Eddy!" Daryl dashes after her. "What do we do now?"

"Fuh…" She wrenches the phone from the mounted wall receiver, getting blood on it, and dials 911. "H…h…here," she finally manages.

"What about our home?" Daryl asks.

Eddy just shakes her head as she falls into a chair and grips her hand over the cut on her wrist.

Half an hour later, Eddy and Daryl are sitting on the parking lot curb with one large blanket over both of their shoulders. The flashing red and blue of a cop car nearby is illuminating the night; the Fog has drifted off slightly. A portable set of floodlights is set up at their apartment door and emergency responders from the Department of Nonhuman Affairs are voiding out the old goodly charm and constructing a new one in its place. Eddy is embarrassed, upset, tired. She leans her head against Daryl's shoulder.

"It's not your fault," he whispers.

Eddy doesn't respond.

Their wrists are bandaged up, and the night is too cold for this. It's also so late, too late. It's past three in the morning, and Eddy has to be at work at nine. She yawns.

"I'm gonna give fronting over to Noah."

"Noah? Why? I don't think—"

"We're fine now. The cops and DNA are here. Sorry, Eddy. I'm about to fall asleep in the headspace, so fronting is gonna jump to him anyways. He's the only one still awake inside right now."

"But—"

"He's with me right now. It's fine. You can reassure him. Or maybe I will." They fall silent.

Eddy raises her head. "Noah?"

"Yeah," he says in a very quiet voice.

"Daryl's with you in the headspace?"

"Yeah. He's...he's on my bed. He said he's gonna fall asleep in a minute. But, but I can't sleep. I never can, and they always do this to me." He shakes his head.

"Do what?"

"They fall asleep when the body doesn't want to fall asleep, and then I'm pushed out, and I can't sleep either already, so now..." He sniffs. "Now I probably won't sleep until tomorrow night."

"Noah..." Eddy rubs his back. "I'm sorry. I didn't...I didn't know you have trouble sleeping."

"Here especially. This new place. It's so hard." Noah sniffs again and rubs a hand over his eye.

"It's okay, Noah. Just don't think about it right now. The DNA people are almost done. Then we can get back into the apartment, and everything will be fine."

Noah shakes his head again.

Eddy keeps rubbing his back as Noah cries silently and fidgets every now and then.

Time passes so slowly, and Eddy desperately wishes they would hurry up. Tomorrow is going to be dreadful if she doesn't get enough sleep.

She starts to zone out. The flashing police lights fade out, and she's only really listening to the slight breeze rustling through the branches of trees. Her mind drifts listlessly across memories and thoughts. She feels displaced, and a vivid recollection of home materializes in her mind.

Not her home now, with Adrastos and the apartment, but before, in the city on the state border south of here with her father. It's about ninety miles by car, over a bridge and west of downtown. That's how to get home…

Noah flails his arm sideways into Eddy's chest.

"Ay! Noah." Her dozing is dispelled, and she grabs his shoulder to keep Noah from falling over on the curb.

"S-sorry. I had a dream. Of home before. With…Mom."

"Noah, it's fine." Eddy rubs an eye. "Just a dream. You started falling asleep."

Noah starts rocking back and forth. "Why do they never go away?"

"Glendower? Eduardo?" The cop walks up with a clipboard in his hand.

Noah fidgets again and looks straight down at the ground.

"Yeah," Eddy says, looking up at him. "That's…us."

"The emergency DNA responders are almost finished. Charm's repainted and they'll give you access again before they leave."

"Are they doing a rapprochement too? To make sure it's safe inside?"

"A rapproch—? Oh, right. It's a 'voiding' now. That's what DNA calls it."

"So, it's…the same thing?"

"No, it's a voiding. They said everything will be just fine."

"Okay…whichever. Just so long as we'll be safe from the ghosts in the Fog."

"The *entities* in the Fog." The cop looks down at his clipboard and starts writing something. "Who's the head of the household?"

"Um, both of us?"

"Right. I'll just put you down, Eduardo."

"Um, I prefer Eddy."

"Right, right. This is the official paper work, so it's Eduardo on here."

A woman wearing a tan work jumpsuit with DNA emblazoned on the breast pocket walks up. "These the two residents?" she asks.

"Yep." The cop nods.

The woman puts her hands on her hips. "That was a right stupid thing you did. Blood on a charm? Crude, prehistoric. Not at all a modern solution."

"But why did it fail?" Eddy asks.

The woman hesitates a moment. "It was actually the alcohol in your blood. But even if your blood had been clean as a whistle, it still would have been nothing more than a stopgap."

"We're all finished here though?" The cop asks her. "I just have to finish this paper work."

"Yes. Everything done to the letter on our end. We checked the place out and nothing got in, so we didn't have to do a voiding. We'll have the forms in the mail by tomorrow. Good night." She turns to leave.

"Wait, wait." Eddy wants to stand, but she doesn't trust her knees to stop shaking. "You—you *didn't* do a voiding?"

The woman halts. "No. The place checked out."

"But…are you sure?"

"Yes. We know how to do our job. *Good night.*" She leaves.

The cop just shakes his head. "They don't have licenses for nothing. Now, you're being fined for the repainting."

"W-what?" Eddy jerks her head to him. "But, but—*what*?"

"Tampering with city property and repairs accrued."

"N-no. No, no, no. We can't. We…" Eddy stands now, the blanket falling away from her. Her knees are shaking, but she isn't even thinking about them right now. "We can't. *Why*?"

The cop holds up a hand. "Official policy. Since the Metaphysical Consolidation Act four years ago, all goodly charms are now utilities and owned by the city or state government, depending on districting. The Department of

Nonhuman Affairs, also created by that act, are the only ones authorized to create, repair, or dissolve any charms and to carry out any related metaphysical services. You tampered with city property and destroyed it in the process. Hence, the fine. It's $380."

"But…we don't have the money for that. We don't."

"Not my problem. In a perfect world, people wouldn't be going around fiddling with stuff they don't know about. There's information on the back about how you can set up payment in installments. Otherwise"—he tears off the fine and hands it to Eddy—"payment is due in full by the end of the month."

I stand here as I
sit here and he says I
am an overlay.
i am not an overlay
i am not, cannot, will not, won;t

i am ahole inside aheart, I
oblong heart, i am ice sliding
back and around, i am behind you

i am.. I am behind, behead
last, amoung us, amoung you,
and i ca

i
i will crawl in your
skin and live in your bones

Splinter 5

The apartment doesn't feel the same.

The door hangs open as Eddy and Noah stand just inside the threshold, the new goodly charm reflecting a heathy bit of light. Nothing about the inside feels wrong right now, but just knowing it had been completely exposed to the outside makes the whole place feel…cracked. Like the rain is going to start seeping in, and the wind will blow its cold breath through the walls.

"It doesn't smell like lilacs," Noah says softly.

"What? Why would it smell like lilacs?"

"Because. One time the grandparents got gremlins in their garage. A shaman came and did a rapprochement to get them out, and it smelled like lilacs for weeks afterward in there."

"They didn't do a rapprochement," Eddy says. "Or a voiding. They didn't do any kind of cleansing. Weren't you listening?"

"…no. But, why not? Why didn't they?"

"They said we didn't need it."

Noah takes one step forward, then backs up again, bumping into Eddy. "They should have done one anyway. To be safe."

"I know. But if they said it's fine, well, it is their line of work. They should know what they're doing. I guess we can just keep an eye on it. But now"—Eddy yawns—"now I have *got* to get to bed. I have work in like…six hours." She walks toward her room.

Noah stays motionless in the main room, his gaze drifting about slowly. "Wait."

"What?"

"How are we going to pay that fine?"

Eddy opens her mouth slightly, then turns her head down. There are a few leaves on the carpet, green and fresh. The DNA responders must have let them blow in when they were working.

Eddy shakes her head. "I dunno."

"Maybe our biograndparents. Or our manager. At the mattress store. He—he might give us an advance. On our pay."

"We'll figure it out, okay? We will. We have to."

Noah lifts his chin as if he were about to nod, but instead he just yawns.

"I'll see you in the morning. I'm gonna die tomorrow if I don't get some sleep." Eddy starts back to her room.

"Can I…can I sleep in your bed tonight with you?" He's wringing his hands.

Eddy stops and returns to Noah, smiling slightly. "Yeah. Yeah, Noah." She squeezes his shoulder. "Come on. We'll be fine."

The next morning Eddy gets to work late and is so much more tired than usual. She is sluggish at her tables, and her tips begin to reflect that fact. But now she needs that money more than ever, and splinters of worry keep worming into her mind, setting off small cascades of panic. She messes up the orders for her next three tables.

Even after bumping up the tips she's getting, this day is still looking really bad money-wise.

Her last table is some small respite. It's a small family: mother, father, and a daughter visiting from college. It's the father's birthday, so they've mostly been wrapped up in conversation, and Eddy has been able to focus her effort on finishing up her remaining tables without needing to keep attending the birthday table.

As Eddy's other tables each finish and trickle out of the restaurant, she's finally able to breathe a sigh of relief for getting through the shift. That feeling is short-lived. Karyn—one of the front of house managers, second in command—pulls Eddy aside.

"Eddy, what's up today? You're usually not this sloppy."

"I'm sorry. It's nothing, really. Just…a rough night last night." Eddy looks away. "Didn't get much sleep."

Karyn crosses her arms. "Have some coffee or something. There's really no excuse for you to be making this many mistakes."

"Yes, ma'am. I'm sorry."

"Remember, we're trying to run a perfect restaurant here. You're not normally on my radar, Eddy, but consider this your verbal warming, got it?"

"Yeah. I got it. Perfect restaurant."

Karyn walks away, and Eddy rubs her temples. She's still so tired. "Fuck today," she mutters.

The birthday family is finished eating, and Eddy quickly clears off their table, the stack of dishes swaying slightly in her hands, but she rights it and chuckles nervously.

"These plates. They're just, trying to get away from me, you know?" She forces a smile.

The father doesn't look amused. "I want to see a dessert menu."

"Of course, of course. I'll be right back."

Earlier, the daughter had arrived before her father to drop off a small bakery cake done up with frosting and candles. Eddy was a bit miffed; that was extra money they wouldn't be spending, extra money that wouldn't go toward increasing her tip. But this was her last table, so she was going to get it perfect.

She retrieves the cake from the walk-in refrigerator and lights the candles. Eddy returns to the table, cake displayed as she sets it before the father with a smile.

"What is this?" he asks. "Am I eight years old?"

The mother and daughter laugh. "It's for your birthday," the daughter says.

"I'll be right back with some dessert plates for you." Eddy leaves, and the mother and daughter start singing "Happy Birthday."

When Eddy returns less than a minute later, the cake has been pushed aside and the mother and daughter are no longer smiling. Eddy isn't even able to put down the plates before the father speaks.

"I want a real dessert. Bring me the dessert menu."

Eddy hesitates. "I—I'm sorry?"

"Bring me a dessert menu. I don't want this." He points to the cake.

Eddy glances at the daughter, but she doesn't say anything. She just sits there, biting her lower lip, her eyes averted.

"Um, I'll—I'll be just a moment." Eddy leaves the three plates stacked on the table.

At the service station Eddy doesn't move. She has dessert menus in her hand, but she doesn't go back. Not yet. What can she do? How could she possibly make this better? It's not her place; it's not possible. The other servers continue working around her, some of them already gone because lunch shift is almost over. They have their own tables, their own problems. She doesn't want to go back.

Eddy approaches the table slowly and gives a menu to the man. "Um, do you want one?" Eddy asks the mother.

Both she and the daughter shake their heads.

Eddy starts to turn away, but the man says, "Don't leave. I just need a second."

She waits and says nothing.

"Here," he points at the menu. "Bring me the skillet cookie with ice cream."

"Chocolate or vanilla?"

"Vanilla." He holds the menu up to her.

"Okay." She takes the menu. "It'll be out in—in a bit."

Eddy sends in the dessert order and feels so unsure of herself now. Everything's going wrong, and it's not her fault. The dessert comes up, and she brings it out to that man.

"Much better." He digs into it with his spoon.

The daughter is no longer at the table.

Later he finishes, having eaten it all. He asks for the cake to be reboxed and the mother pays the bill. Eddy doesn't take any extra money.

That evening Eddy is back home, back at the apartment. Adrastos is at the mattress store where they work, and Eddy wishes she wasn't alone right now. She stands in the main room and rubs her elbow. Does the apartment really feel different now? Slowly Eddy rotates her head, surveying the main room. If anything, it looks…smaller somehow. Like the room has more furniture in it than before, even though that certainly isn't the case.

She wanders into her room in the silent apartment, and sits cross-legged on her bed. How are they going to pay that fine? They only have a few weeks. On the back of the ticket it says they can go to the downtown Department of Nonhuman Affairs branch and set up a monthly payment plan, but they have to do that within ten days of receiving the fine. As soon as Eddy gets her schedule for next week she'll have to find time to go do that, considering it's her name on the bill. If she and Adrastos can just get through this month then everything will be fine. They'll get settled on their feet and be able to move forward with their lives.

With a deep sigh, Eddy picks up her tarot cards to consult them. She shuffles the deck, letting her mind be blank and open to the cards. She cuts and deals three out in a row.

Five of Pentacles. Nine of Swords. Seven of Swords.

She frowns. "Thanks a lot, cards."

Eddy sets them aside and flops back on her bed, staring up at the ceiling. A slight headache drifts through the back of her mind, and after several minutes of empty thoughts Eddy thinks that maybe it wouldn't be *that* bad if she had to go back home. Go back and live with her father. But she shakes her head. No, no. She left for a reason. No point backtracking in life.

Eddy starts to doze off, but then she hears something.

Water.

The apartment does have a leak. Eddy knew it. She sits straight up in bed and closes her eyes, straining her ears. She doesn't know where it is, or what exactly is leaking, but she can hear it. The plinking of falling drops, the soft gushing of water through pipes. Where is it?

"*Al jacal viejo no le faltan goteras*," she mumbles. It's one of the sayings her mother often used to quote: an old house doesn't lack for leaks.

She hops out of bed and checks the likely places: under the sink, under the refrigerator. None of the cabinets have anything promising. She can't even find any water. Perhaps the leak is inside the walls? Slowly eating away at the plaster, saturating the insulation, growing a forest of mushrooms. The spores could be floating through the air vents right now. They could settle in her lungs, and one day she would simply wake up in the dark of the morning unable to breathe, drowning above water.

Eddy presses her ear against the wall in the kitchen, but the sound fades out. She pulls away and can hear it again, the running of water. If only Adrastos was here. They could've helped her find the problem.

She closes her eyes and listens.

Water is flowing softly somewhere. Where? The bathroom?

She should check. But Eddy doesn't move yet. She stands frozen. Waiting. Nothing. The sound is slowly draining away.

Finally Eddy moves. The bathroom is just a few feet away, but the distance seems farther. She flicks the light switch, and the bulb flashes on too bright, blindingly bright, and bursts with a pop. Eddy gasps and steps back, fumbling behind her, trying to grab the wall. She touches it and leans against the plaster to catch her breath, but it doesn't return. The air's been squeezed out of her, and instead a cough starts welling up in her lungs, forcing them to spasm. Cold washes over her; tendrils of goose bumps crawling across her body, flowing beneath her clothes.

She coughs and coughs and squeezes her eyes shut, trying to focus on something, anything. She grasps at words so infrequently repeated but can't arrange them into the orison in her mind. *Circled—circled by the, circled by—by—circled by—the—the goodly, circled by, the charms. Cradled—cradled by…*

The coughing does not stop.

us poor now, sou s now,us here now
I am here away from here.
I will spit out bi e, not water, not
        blood
i can an overlay, a over stock,
overstuffed like a mattresss bloated bogged
down with rainwater drown as the dirt it
swells through, over lay lines and
painted lines, powerlines, cords tangled
undergrounf, under dirt, under me,
around coiling
        me, inside,
coilding,reaching

i

//I/wyw/ why???

you and i forced i
inside

coiling inside with powerlines.

Splinter 6

Eddy is at work? She's been sat eight tables at the same time, and she's panicking. There's no way she can do this. There's no one to help her. She's going to be fired. The restaurant is normally split into two main dining areas by a wall dividing the building, but they have removed it temporarily because it's overdue for its yearly painting. Eddy can see every table she hasn't greeted yet. Every guest without even water. It's too many. It's impossible.

One of them, a man sitting in a booth by himself, cannot and will not wait anymore. He picks up his knife and starts scraping it against the table, curling up long shavings of wood. He sneers at Eddy and keeps scraping, keeps scraping. The knife is about to break through the table; the man is about to start scraping through the skin on his leg. Deliberately.

"Eddy."

She wakes up, and Adrastos is standing over her bed. She gasps and pulls the blanket up over her bare chest, a habit that has always come naturally even though she doesn't actually have breasts.

"Adrastos! What are you doing?"

"It's just me, Daryl." He's standing with his shoulders forward, head slightly hunched, and hands deep in his pocket. He's not wearing a shirt.

"Oh. Okay." Eddy lowers the blanket and sits up. "Why are you scaring me like that?"

"Didn't mean to." He's silent a second. "Sorry."

"It's okay." Eddy rubs her eyes and blinks a few times. A certain clamminess starts crawling across her skin now that the covers aren't over her. "So, what's up? What do you want?"

Daryl sits on the edge of the bed and leans back, lying on top of her legs. "Noah wanted me to ask you something." He turns his head to face her. "Do you think the apartment feels any better?"

"What?"

"You know. Like…" He glances away for a moment, rubbing his top teeth against his bottom lip. "Like not weird anymore."

"Um…" Something is really nagging her now. Something is slinking around beneath her thoughts, lumping them up like mole tunnels, sending aching pulses through her brain. Eddy rubs a temple. "He means because there's no lilacs."

"I guess."

Eddy sighs. "I really don't know. I—I kind of don't think there's anything. I mean, I feel a little restless, but nothing really besides that."

"He says it feels like something's out of place."

They just look at each other for a moment.

"Can you get up, Daryl? My legs are falling asleep."

"Sorry." He sits up.

Eddy gets out of bed. She's only wearing a pair of briefs, but she doesn't mind if it's only Daryl in the room with her. She goes to her small walk-in closet and Daryl watches her.

"Noah won't stop mentioning it," he says, "and I feel kinda restless too. Like I had my den, but then it got all trampled up by someone else and feels"—he lifts his hands and flexes his fingers a few times, as if squeezing something—"feels like mud tracks over my bed, making it not my bed anymore."

"What about the others?" Eddy asks from the closet.

"None of them front enough to notice it." Daryl is silent a moment. "Did you know the bathroom light is broken?"

"No. What happened?"

"I dunno. I found it broken, and we cleaned it up."

Eddy steps out with a shirt and pulls it on but still feels cold. "I'll go down to the office and put in a work order for a new light bulb."

Daryl is silent a moment. "What do you feel?"

"What?"

"Noah wants to know what you feel."

Eddy takes in a deep breath and holds it before exhaling. "I think…I think we're just too stressed out right now. You know, from moving in and from that fine and living on our own…All that stuff."

Daryl shakes his head. "I wish. I want to have something I can target." He closes his eyes and presses two fingers from each hand against his eyelids.

"Don't do that." Eddy grabs his wrists and pulls his hands away gently.

Daryl just looks at his hands in hers. "Sorry," he says very softly. "I…don't even notice, notice when I'm doing that."

"It's okay. Just—just don't do that." She lowers his hands but keeps holding them.

He looks away. "I keep the body safe. And something's wrong."

"I think…maybe"—Eddy licks her lips—"maybe they really should have done a voiding."

"Yeah."

"Look, I have to go to the DNA branch anyways to work out a payment plan. When I go I'll find out about getting some sort of, I dunno, follow-up. Someone to recheck the place. It's all gonna be fine, okay? We just have to get through this month."

Daryl shakes his head. "I want my teeth back."

"I know. I know." She squeezes his hands. "Do you guys work today?"

"No."

"Let Harold front when I go down to the apartment office."

Shortly after, Eddy is standing at the open apartment door, looking out into the light drizzle of rain falling over the world. Her umbrella is broken somehow since the move. The clasp won't hold the stretchers out and keep them locked in place. Technically the thing still works, but it demands two hands now and constant effort just to keep up the protective dome. Eddy sighs.

The clamminess is still under her skin. Not even a warm shower has shaken it. She chalks it up to anxiety.

Holding the umbrella open, Eddy crosses the apartment complex to the office building. Only one person is in the front room, occupying one of the three desks. A coffee machine sits in the corner only half-filled, the rest of the pot stained light brown from the countless brews before.

The man behind the desk looks up and smiles. "Good morning. Keeping dry?"

Eddy kind of nods and shrugs at the same time by tilting her head to the side and raising one shoulder. "Mostly. Umbrella's a bit broken." She lets go of the clasp and the umbrella folds inward.

"Sorry to hear about that. So what can I help you with today?" He swivels his chair away from a brand-new boxy computer to fully face Eddy. He's got short black hair, glasses, nice eyes. Eddy thinks he's cute, even though he's older than what she'd normally be interested in. Probably midthirties.

"Well, I, uh, I need two things." She sits down. "First I need a work order."

"Not for the umbrella, I hope." He smiles again.

A small grin forces its way across Eddy's face. "No, no. It's for a new light bulb. Also, I need to know what sort of contracting with DNA is covered by the apartment complex."

"Everything except tampering, we cover. If you're here about that disturbance a few days ago, rest assured we were informed and are deciding on the proper course of action."

"Wh-what disturbance?" Eddy asks.

"Oh, you're not asking about that? The disturbance at three in the morning when someone ruined their goodly charm and had to call the emergency responders. We've already gotten numerous complaints."

Eddy doesn't know what to say. She feels her skin tightening across her body and takes too long to reply.

"Are you alright? You suddenly look sick."

"That…that was…me."

"What?"

"Apartment ten-fifteen. That's us. That's why I'm here."

"Ooooh. Well then." The man leans forward on his elbows and laces his fingers together. "We were informed you were fined for the event. This community really does frown on such failure to adhere to DNA code. You could be endangering everyone."

"But…but…it wasn't our fault. Our goodly charm—"

"*You* put blood on that goodly charm, not anyone else. The blames seems quite clear-cut here. In a perfect world, we wouldn't be getting any emergency calls to our complex, so what went wrong with you?"

"*Nothing.* Our goodly charm was fading, and then the Fog came that night, and we couldn't get inside without breaking the ward. We had to do something."

"Why were you even outside at three in the morning?"

Eddy looks down at her hands. "We…we went to a bar. Stayed later than we thought…"

The man leans back and drums his fingernails on the table. "Sounds like that was still your choice. Now. What did you want? Why are you here?"

"The—the light bulb, and, DNA. We—we want a follow-up."

"A follow-up? One mistake wasn't enough?"

"No! That's not what I mean. We—I mean, my roommate and I—we don't think the apartment feels the same. We want to make sure it really is okay. They didn't do a voiding, so we want to get the place rechecked."

"They *didn't* do a voiding? I would've thought that'd be a top priority after someone breaks their own charm."

"When they were here that night they said we didn't need it."

"Hmph. Well. I'll give you the paper work, but you better hope everything is all prim and proper with your apartment." He turns away from her and opens a drawer in a filing cabinet. "You understand we will be updated on any findings made by DNA, and it's within our right as a complex to evict anyone found by DNA to be dangerous."

Eddy presses her hands flat on the man's desk. "We're *not* dangerous."

"That will be up to DNA, I should think." He smirks and drops down a small stapled packet of papers. "Now I'm not entirely certain how all these new codes from that legislation work on your end, so I think you'll just have to figure it out yourself. All I know is that it's a lot more paper work on our end than just hiring an independent company like before."

"So…where do I take these?" She points at the packet. "Bring them back to you?"

"No. Take them down to the DNA branch office. You're lucky that they're right downtown since we're the largest city in the county. They'll deal with you from here."

"Well…we also need a normal work order, for a light bulb," she adds in a quiet tone.

"Sure, sure." The man takes out another form. "Fill this out here, and I'll add it to maintenance's in-box."

Eddy fills the work order out quickly and slides it back across the desk. She stands and snaps up the DNA paper work. "You've been such a huge help."

"I don't need your sarcasm. Just go." He waves her out of the office.

"Adrastos!" Eddy calls out as she opens the door to the apartment. "Apparently management hates us now. The guy at the office almost bit my head off."

"What's this? What have you done this time?"

"Me?" Eddy kicks off her shoes. "It's still that goodly charm incident. It's really their fault for not keeping up with repainting them. Who's fronting?"

Adrastos is in the kitchen, intermittently eating a sandwich and unpacking a box. "It's Harold. You told Daryl to let me front, and he actually listened this time."

"Oh. Well, good."

"Now, what is this new development? Daryl and Noah have been keeping me up to speed, so no need to backtrack any of the story."

"Management has been getting complaints about the emergency call that night. Now them and everyone else are suspicious of us, apparently. And it's no good that I came in there asking for DNA paper work!" Eddy slaps the stapled pages down on the kitchen table.

"Ah." Harold holds up a finger but returns to his sandwich.

"That's it from you, too?"

"Afraid so. No good news on our side either."

"What? You mean…did you ask your manager about an advance?"

"Yes. Actually. Daryl didn't mention this?"

"No…What happened?"

Harold clasps his hands behind his back. "Our manager at the mattress store said no."

"That's it?"

"That's it." Harold nods. "Oh, but look! I did find these." He leans down and takes out a frying pan from the cupboard. "Daryl can cook you both chicken pancakes again."

"Come on, Harold, I think we have other things more important to worry about right now. You never tell me the story straight on anything. Should I call on Hanna to give me the short version?"

Harold slips the pan back into the cupboard. "Hmm, let's say no. Definitely no. Her short and blunt would be far too short and blunt." Harold shakes his head. "No, no. Essentially, the essence of the story, the best way for me to distill it—"

"Just spit it out."

"Eddy. Okay." Harold takes a deep breath and puts a finger to his mouth momentarily. "It boils down to the fact that our manager is a little bit *familiar* with 'Glen,' if you know what I mean."

"No…I don't know this. I haven't been told anything about this."

"It's very simple really. What does everyone want? Everyone crave? Of course, we all vetoed the idea instantly. Well, Noah wasn't told because he'd just start crying, and Daryl did give it some consideration at first, but Hanna and I instantly said no." The volume of his voice starts fading back. "No way at all. Our manager was slick with his words, though, let me tell you. He said, 'Nothing I can do for you, Glen. I'm so sorry. You do understand my hands are tied.' Then he said—this was the good part, the slick turn around—'Perhaps something could be done. Maybe something if it was *your* hands tied…' "

Harold's mouth keeps moving, but Eddy can't hear anything anymore. It's just a deep muffled droning coming from far off, like she's listening to him underwater. She blinks several times in rapid succession and wonders absently how long it would take to walk all the way back home.

Eddy is washing her hands at the kitchen sink now and looks up. The Adrastos System is not in the kitchen or in the living room. There are fewer boxes in the kitchen. A mild headache is floating on the surface of her mind.

"Harold?" She calls out.

"No. It's me. Noah." He calls from their room. "What's up?"

Eddy looks down at the cooking sheet next to the sink with rows of premade cookie dough squares atop it. The package for the chocolate chip cookies is nearby and the oven is already preheated. She blinks a few times, and everything is normal.

"I'm putting the cookies in now," she says.

"Wait!" Noah dashes out and takes another square of cookie dough.

"Noah, geez! Stop." She slaps at his hand playfully. "You've had like eight now. There's not going to be any actual cookies if you keep eating these."

"I can't help it. I haven't had dinner yet. I'm hungry."

"It's past ten. Why haven't you eaten yet?"

"I dunno." He yawns and shakes his head. "I didn't even think about it until you got back from the grocery store. I've had a headache since I started fronting, and that's all I've really been thinking about."

Eddy snaps her fingers. "I knew I forgot something at the store. I didn't get any aspirin. Dammit." She rubs one of her temples.

Noah is eyeing the cookie dough again and starts to reach for another piece.

"Stop." She shoos his hand away. "There's some left over mac and cheese in the fridge from when Daryl thought he could eat three boxes at once."

"Oh. I forgot that was a thing."

Noah starts preparing a bowl of macaroni as Eddy puts the cookies in the oven. She closes the oven door and stands. Some sound catches her attention.

Noah starts entering the time in the microwave. *Beep, beep, beep.* "I think it'd be cool if—"

"*Aguas.* Stop, stop. Shush." Eddy raises a hand. "Do you hear that?"

Noah looks at her, his finger hovering over the Start button. "What?"

"Water," Eddy says softly. "I swear I hear water running."

They both stand without making a sound.

"I…no. I don't. I don't hear anything." Noah says.

Eddy sighs. "It stopped." She walks away a few steps.

"Are you sure?"

"Yeah."

"What was it like?"

"Like, just, water flowing. Through a pipe maybe." She puts her hands on her hips and looks up at the ceiling. "Maybe we need to put in another work order. I really hope not, but leaks are a big deal, right?"

"We need to stop the bleeding soon."

"Bleeding?" Eddy looks over her shoulder.

Noah is still looking at the microwave, one hand over his left eye. "You know. Like in a machine. If it's leaking oil and splattering that darkness all over the floor, then fixing it fast can save bigger problems."

"Yeah…that's what I was thinking. 'Bleeding' is just a really dramatic word."

Noah smiles as he turns the microwave on. "Your face is a dramatic word."

Eddy scoffs and pushes his shoulder lightly. "Eat your damn macaroni. The cookies will be done soon."

i will fester in
open sores, open
eyes.
Gorged out by birth-
right and expectent burdens.
Pieces of
me are floateng away
between you, leading to
the place, the peace. bri-
nger collecting..
/ ./
Calling away from
here by your
hands, scratching
out the signs un-
spoken. Ductile and
directed, I /will? not.
I am not. Shatter me.
Rain down gore and mem-
ories and names on reign,
reigning. RUNNINg again
LeaD////ing againn .
I will your lead inhailed
like spores,,
like specks. Coatig yoru
lungs and d row ning the
cold and /curdling/ his
blood.
BLood isn;t thicker if blasted,
mixed, bled out and made as
FERTILIZER. tangling roots and
tendrils will claim your husk
as home, as hearth. /
My mind is already the the
the same as /thIs/.
////
please don't. dont follow

Splinter 7

Eddy tries to go to the local DNA branch that Monday, but the wait time is projected at two hours, and she definitely won't have enough time before she has to be at work. Another day passes. On Wednesday morning Eddy sleeps in a little too late and doesn't arrive before the line builds up. There's only a week left to get a payment plan set up for their fine, so she doesn't have much choice. She takes a number. At least she brought a book.

There's eight windows to help people, but the line moves slowly. For a while Eddy is perfectly fine reading *Infinite Break: The Invisible Emperor*, but slowly the plastic chair becomes increasingly uncomfortable. She ends up shifting around in it more and more as time wears on.

Over forty minutes pass, and while the line is getting closer to her number, it still seems a long way off. Then Eddy hears someone blowing on something across the aisle from her. She glances up.

A black guy, probably close to Eddy's age, is sitting in the opposite chair. His hair is buzzed short, and he's wearing a button-up shirt. He has one of those palm camcorders in his lap, and he's blowing some dust out from the tape holder.

She keeps watching him until he looks up. He smiles, but Eddy feels embarrassed for staring and quickly looks back down at her book. Almost a minute passes, and she look up again with her eyes. He's still looking at her, and he raises his eyebrows.

"Long wait, isn't it?" he says.

"Oh. Yeah. Yeah, it is."

"What number do you have?"

"Um." Eddy pulls the ticket from her pocket. "D84."

"I've got B37. I wonder what the letters mean." He puts his ticket in his breast pocket.

"I dunno. Maybe different departments?"

"Maybe."

He glances down at his camcorder, and they both don't say anything else. Eddy wants to say something else, but she also wants to keep reading. But not really. She likes his smile.

She will tell him her name. She plans this in her mind, knows it's only two words to utter, but somehow this takes more effort than what she's already said. I'm Eddy. That's what she'll say. I'm Eddy.

"I'm Eddy."

"Philip." He stands up halfway and leans forward so they can shake hands across the aisle. "What are you reading?"

"This? Oh, it's just—just this pulp fantasy series with time travel." She stops, but realizes saying more would give Philip more to work with. She adds a bit quickly, "It's not highbrow reading at all but, you know, I really like the characters."

"I can understand that." He nods. "How many books are in it?"

"Five right now. The sixth one is coming out soon, so I'm rereading them."

"And what's the sixth one called?"

"*The Forgotten Year.*" Eddy has the book closed now, just one finger between the pages to keep her place.

"And that's the time travel?"

"Yeah. It's—it's nerdy, I know."

Philip chucks softly. "I know about being a nerd." He raises the camcorder slightly.

"Well…yeah." Eddy looks at the camcorder and back up at Philip. "I'm actually a little worried about the new book."

"What do you mean?"

"Oh, I mean, overall I think she's done the time travel really well. Hasn't made it too weird. Especially since the time travel is a central thing. But, you see, this one I'm reading right now, the fourth book, is actually were it starts to get more wonky than normal. And the fifth, *The Dark Mirror*, is the, well, the least good, really. I just really, really hope that she doesn't drag out the mirror kingdom stuff, because it's pretty bad. If she can just wrap it up real fast in the first quarter of the next book and focus on the main character's child more, then I think it'll be way better." Eddy stops and forces a smile. "Sorry."

"I don't mind." Philip shakes his head. "Is, uh, is that seat taken?" He points to the chair next to Eddy.

She glances at it, then sits up a little more. "No. It isn't."

Philip smiles as he sits down next to Eddy. Neither of them know what else to say for a moment, but both of them know they can't broach the topic of why they're here in the DNA branch.

"Why'd you bring a camcorder?" Eddy asks.

"I almost always have it on me. Ever since high school really, when I took my first filming class. It's just something I like. I'm almost always thinking in filming mode too, so actually having my camcorder is useful for that."

"What do you mean, 'filming mode?' "

"You know, like shots and angles. If I was making a movie, how would I compose this scene? How would I create the right look? That kind of stuff."

"Cool. I've never met someone who does filming."

Philip nods. "Well, I've never actually filmed anything before. Like no movies or anything."

"I know, I mean, I didn't expect you to be in Hollywood."

"No." Philip forces a bit of a smile. "But what I mean is I haven't really made anything complete. No short films. I've never even worked with actors before. Just scenery, kind of. Like, I guess you could say I'm too focused on the colors and not the painting itself."

"Oh." Eddy thinks a moment. "That's not bad though, right? It's like practice."

"Yeah, kinda." He shrugs.

They're both silent again. Another number gets called out, this one very close to Eddy's number. She looks back up at Philip.

"So what kind of camera is that?"

"It's a Video8 camcorder. It's close to eight years old, this thing. My uncle gave it to me. Do you know this is the first handheld model they ever made?" He pauses. "Do you want to see it?" He holds the camcorder up.

"Oh! I—I mean, that sounds like it's really, you know, important to you. I wouldn't want to break it." Eddy shakes her head.

Philip chuckles. "You're not gonna break it by holding it. I trust you."

Eddy opens her mouth slightly, wanting to say something in response. He can't know that, can't know that he trusts her. She wants to say that he can't know that after just a few minutes. She takes the camcorder.

It's fairly bulky, even for a non-shoulder-mounted camcorder. It's mostly just a large black rectangle with a second gray piece attached to the side that holds the battery, viewfinder, and microphone.

"Push that button to record." Philip leans over and points to a red button.

"Okay."

The button sticks a moment, but then the camcorder whirrs, and a few small lights turn on. Eddy raises the camcorder to her eye and looks around the room with a few passes.

"Neat, huh?" Philip asks.

Eddy turns the camcorder to him, looking at his face framed in the viewfinder. He's smiling with such nice white teeth, his head tilted a little to the side.

"It is," she whispers.

A new number is called out, Eddy's number. She lowers the camcorder and turns it off.

"That's me. I, uh, I guess I gotta go."

"Wait." Philip tugs on his ear a moment. "Can I have your phone number?"

Eddy blinks in surprise, then nods. "Y-yeah. Sure. Yeah. Do you have a pen?"

Philip feels his pockets for a moment. "No, but I got something else. Let me have the camcorder."

Eddy gives it back, and Philips holds it up, the lens now focused on her. "Just tell me your number on film."

"That's smart." Eddy smiles. "I'm at 360-555-0108."

"Thanks. I'll call you soon."

The DNA clerk processing Eddy's paper work is an older woman. Her hair is white and pulled up into a bun, and she wears glasses connected to a beaded necklace cord. She's typing into one of those new office computers.

She leans forward to check a piece of information on the papers Eddy brought. "Yes, I know this apartment complex. Not far from here at all. Just a few roads over if I remember correctly." Her voice is old and a bit scratchy.

"Close enough to walk." Eddy nods.

"Now, about this request you're filing…" She speaks slowly, and picks up a cigarette from the ashtray on her desk. "Our records show that a voiding wasn't necessary."

"Yeah, but we think we need one."

The woman sighs. "Okay. Let's put that one to the side for now. This other form you brought…it's for payment?"

Eddy just nods and slides the fine forward. "This one."

The woman adjusts her glasses and is silent for several minutes as she works on the computer. "Yes…tampering with your goodly charm. Not a smart idea at all." She shakes her head.

"I didn't mean to."

"Ah, ah, ah." The woman shakes her finger. "The road to Hel is paved with good intentions."

Eddy grunts and crosses her arms. She didn't come here to get more lectures.

"The payment plans we can offer you right now are four months at one hundred-one dollars and ninety-nine cents each, six months at sixty-nine fifty-five each, eight months at fifty-three forty-five each, or twelve months at thirty-five ninety-nine. Which one will you take?"

"Wait—wait. What? I didn't—didn't get all that."

The woman sighs and stubs out her cigarette. "I'll just print it out for you." She types something into the computer, then hobbles away from her desk with the help of a cane, leaving Eddy alone for several minutes.

Eddy leans forward on her elbows. She wants to start reading again while the woman is gone, but Eddy isn't sure how long she'll be away. About five minutes pass, and Eddy cracks her book open, but not another ten seconds go by before the DNA clerk returns.

"Here. Choose your rate and start filling out that form as I enter this other request into the system." She gives Eddy two papers.

Eddy doesn't spend much time looking over the different rates: $35.99 each month is really the only safe option for her and Adrastos. The payment being stretched over twelve months is concerning to her, but Eddy doesn't think they really have a choice. She begins filling out the form.

After a short time, then DNA clerk looks up and says, "Now, let me make sure I'm understanding this claim here. The responders who repainted your goodly charm also checked out the apartment but found the location to be safe and therefore didn't carry out a voiding. However, you are now claiming that a voiding *is* necessary, but on this form here you haven't listed a single symptom of a possible incursion."

"Well…yeah. But—but none of the check boxes really applied to us. There's not really something, uh, specifically wrong."

The woman closes her eyes for several moments and lights up another cigarette. "Let's just double-check. Any strange noises?"

"Just a leaky pipe."

"No cold spots?"

"No."

"Voices?"

"No."

"Nightmares?"

"Uh, not more than normal." Eddy shakes her head.

The clerk nods. "You're not building a strong case for yourself."

"Well, what do you want? We broke our charm, okay, fine. But we think DNA didn't do everything they should have."

The woman chuckles. "The department doesn't often accept these kinds of liabilities. Our contractors are trained for their job, so it seems highly unlikely that they would miss something. It's not often that final diagnoses get overturned so a case can be reopened."

"Can't you just have a shaman come out and, you know, just, look at the place?" Eddy starts flexing the cheap pen supplied to her between her fingers on her lap.

"We don't have shamans anymore. We're a little more advanced now." She smacks her lips together a few times. "They're DNA contractors."

"But, then, who fulfills that role? If there aren't shamans, then who are the attuned people who can handle those metaphysical things?"

She sighs. "Did you even read the pamphlet at the entrance? Freelance shamans, gothi, and others of similar orders are being absorbed into the more systematic approach of the Department of Nonhuman Affairs. All spiritual practices are of course encouraged within the privacy and safety of your own home, but our voidings and treatments are carried out by our singular text. A sort of 'synthesis' never reached before now."

"Right," Eddy says softly.

"So, 'contractors.' That's what they are now. They do the same things, just using a difference approach."

The pen snaps in Eddy's hands. Not intentional. She drops it on the floor. "Then, let's get a contractor out, right?"

"I can't just send someone out." The woman twirls her hand around with the cigarette, then takes another puff from it. "We'd be swamped with false claims about creaky attics and cults in the forest if we just sent people out. You wouldn't believe how often we get—"

"But this isn't some 'false claim' like el Cucuy. This is a voiding that didn't even get done. This is a real thing in a real place."

"Now, now, calm down. There is admittedly a certain element of intuition, along with corroboration." She finishes the second cigarette. "Do you live by yourself?"

"No. I have a roommate."

"And does your roommate feel similarly about the lack of a voiding?"

"Yes. It was the first thing he said when we came back into the apartment afterward."

The older woman nods slowly. "Perhaps we should check just one more thing." She stands up. "I'll be back."

This is probably going to take all day. Eddy slouches in her chair, and then reaches forward to take another pen from the holder near the computer.

"Here." The clerk returns with a large book and starts leafing through its pages. "Now. Any unexplained accumulations of sawdust?"

"Uh, no."

"Damage to mounted pictures or picture frames?"

"No? What are you asking me about?"

"Esoteric symptoms. Next, hearing different lyrics in a song you know very well?"

"No."

"Writing notes, such as grocery lists, and then being unable to read them later?"

"No…are—are these real things?"

She just looks up at Eddy for a moment before saying, "Unfortunately."

"Okay, so these are what? Esoteric symptoms? What are you reading them from? Why aren't they on the normal form?"

"Because it's the normal form. This is a copy of the Alduer Ljósemannt. It's a compilation of the most effective cures for all known metaphysical sickness. Everything is in here, except for your problem, apparently." She smirks a moment.

"But—"

The older woman just holds up a hand and flips a few pages over. "Perhaps one last test."

"I thought that was the last thing."

"One last, last thing then." She slides her finger over one of the pages as she mutters something Eddy can't possibly catch. Then the woman holds the book up to Eddy. "What do you see?"

"In the book?"

"Yes. What do you see?"

"There's…there's just a few splotches of ink on the page."

"Good, good. How many?"

"Um." Eddy leans forward a bit. "Four."

"How dark?"

"Dark?"

"Yes. How dark is the ink? Is it gray? Black? Darker?"

"But you were just looking at the page yourself."

"Just answer this last question, and then I'll explain it." She taps a finger on the page. "How dark?"

"Two of them are black. One's kind of a dark gray, kinda close to black. The last one is like medium-light gray, I guess."

The older woman nods a moment and takes out another cigarette but doesn't light it yet. "That page you just saw has some metaphysical properties. It reflects suppressed memories."

"What? I have—I have suppressed memories?"

"It's not as uncommon as you might think," she says softly as her eyes drift down to the still-open page. "Certain entities can force memory suppression as part of their hunting, yes, but there are also documented cases of certain…fail-safes in the Human mind. A small number of things are too, you might say, great. Too overpowering. Forgetting is the only way to live at times."

"So, I don't understand. Why did you think you needed to test me for suppressed memories?"

"You came in complaining about a problem that you didn't know anything about. Seemed like a good idea. They do train us on these things."

"Wait…so…"

"Try not to worry about it. I'll go ahead and finish submitting your claim. With what you've told me, I think a rediagnosis will certainly be granted. A contractor will be over soon."

"That's it?"

"On your end at least. Just finish up those forms please." She turns to the computer. "Go call your parents tonight. Get reconnected. Take your mind off all this."

Expanse Two

Splinter 8

Eddy frets over both the ink splotches and Philip for the whole walk back to the apartment. She's worried slightly more about Philip, though. *What if he calls tonight? What will I say to him? What will we talk about? Is he* actually *interested in me? Will he still be interested when he finds out?* Her thoughts flit back to the splotches a few times more, but each time comes more slowly than the last, and each time she spends less time holding the subject on the surface of her thoughts.

As she walks, Eddy spots a penny on the sidewalk and doesn't hesitate to pick it up. She squeezes it tight in the palm of her hand the rest of the way.

Back in the apartment Eddy drops the penny into the change cup on the kitchen counter. Hanna is fronting, and she's lounging on the couch with the TV on, even though she's hardly paying attention to it. She isn't too interested in talking about the DNA claim, either.

"But this Philip sounds perfect for you," Hanna says as she keeps flipping through the same eight TV channels like she expects one of them to become something different. "That trip to the office branch wasn't for nothing after all."

"*Nothing*? I have holes in my memory."

"Yes, yes, but he said he's going to call you. If you two go on a date you should—"

"Gods, Hanna, you can't just ignore what they said at the DNA branch because you want to pair me with this guy I just met. This is really serious." Eddy heads toward her bedroom and adds in a more quiet voice, "He probably was only interested because he thinks I'm a guy."

Hanna shifts on the couch, crossing her legs the other way. "Technically, you are. You can just go the Daryl route and sleep with him for a while before cutting him off."

Eddy turns around. "But I want something more than that."

Hanna just shrugs. "Either way. As for the apartment, I, for one, haven't seen anything around here. I'm quite sure Noah is just being a little bitch again."

"You shouldn't be so mean to him. He's really sensitive."

"You don't even know the half of it!" She claps her hands together. "The absolute best part, though, is how delightfully funny it is to see Daryl bristle all up when I chuck those insults Noah's way." She flashes a wide grin.

"Can I just talk to Noah? I need to tell him what happened."

Hanna raises her shoulders and sighs theatrically, flipping the back of her hand over her forehead. "Can't an old woman have an evening to relax? An evening without your parties and formal dressing and casual meetings between such tycoons who want to rule the world?"

"Dammit, Hanna." Eddy rubs her temples.

She continues on with practiced ease. "Such a life as a perfect house-wife. Your trophy and tribute. Your shield against the tribunal of boards and directors and CEOs you seek to topple. Alas, my role gains no credit, no just deserts, nothing so glamorous as your ladder-cracking pyramid schemes, my dear. Never once do you consider my station, my—"

"Are you done yet?" Eddy cuts in.

She titters and stands from the couch, sweeping out her arms and bowing gracefully a few times. "You should hear my *Macbeth*."

Eddy winces. "Don't say that."

"We're not in a theater."

"Doesn't matter."

Hanna simply rolls her eyes. "Then, I quit. I quit this stage and this play! Find a new Kathleen!" She spins around and loses balance, falling sideways onto the couch.

"Why does she have to do that?" Noah asks from the cushions.

"Because she's too dramatic for her own good." Eddy holds out a hand to him.

"I'll stay here." Noah pulls his legs up and tucks himself into the corner between the arm rest and the back of the couch. "So. What did they say?"

Eddy sits next to him, leaning forward with elbows on her knees and hands folded. "Well, it took some convincing, but they agreed to send someone out to recheck the place. Also we owe $35 a month for the next year to them."

"That's not bad. We can do that."

Eddy nods as her gaze drifts away.

"So…you met someone at DNA?" Noah asks.

"Yeah, I did, but…well, I dunno."

"What?"

"I don't think it'll work out."

Noah starts twirling a strand of hair around one finger. "It might."

Eddy shrugs. "It's not important. When I was there at DNA, the lady who was helping me was really hesitant to send someone out. She didn't believe we needed a voiding because we didn't have any symptoms of anything. But they had this book, this Alduer, um, Alduer something, I can't remember. Anyways, there's a metaphysical page that can detect if you have lapses in your memory. It said I have four."

Noah looks up at her. "What does that mean?"

"They don't know. The lady said it could be a few different things, but that I shouldn't worry about it. Maybe I'm just getting early Alzheimer's." Eddy forces a chuckle.

"No. I'm sure you're fine."

"Yeah? Thanks." She pokes his shoulder. "But, anyways, with the symptoms they want. Has anything felt different for you lately? Has there been anything…concrete?"

"I thought you agreed," Noah says softly.

"Noah, that's not what I'm asking. I'm asking if there's anything more. Because all we have now for sure is a few holes in my memory. The weird feeling in here is, well, it's not always there. We don't actually have anything to point to. What if it's us? I mean, like, what if we're just getting paranoid over nothing?"

"I know…" Noah says quietly. "But I know I feel something now. I don't know what, slash, or where. It's so much harder to sleep in the place now at night, in the dark. It just doesn't feel like home anymore."

Eddy pats his shoulder gently. "Okay. We're going to be fine. I promise. Someone's coming. We'll get this sorted out."

The next day Eddy spends most of the morning sitting by the wall-mounted telephone, waiting. The Adrastos System is off at the mattress store. Eddy is reading *Infinite Break* again, waiting. It seems too quiet in the apartment now, and she can't focus. She sets the book down and looks up. Not at anything in particular. Just looking.

Eddy needs something to be in the silence. Something to distract her. She turns on the kitchen sink and stands there for a minute, watching the running water.

Kssssssssss.

She glances over at the phone again and then returns to her book, leaving the water running.

A while passes.

At lunchtime Eddy starts boiling water for ramen. The box of packaged ramen is running low. For a moment she wonders why she didn't pick up another box when she was at the store last time; then she remembers splurging on that cookie dough. She mutters a soft curse.

The phone rings.

Eddy jumps, dropping the ramen packet. She rushes to grab the phone from its receiver.

"Hello?" she asks.

The line is silent.

"Hello?" she asks again.

"Can you hear me?"

"Hey, yeah," Eddy says. "Who is this?"

"This is Philip. Um, is Eddy there?"

"Yeah, this is her."

"Her?"

"Oh. I mean, I'm here. Hey. Uh, how are you?"

"I'm fine. Are you—are you at home? There seems to be a lot of background noise."

Eddy glances over her shoulder. "Oh. That's probably the water. I left it on." She goes back to the sink, stretching the phone cord.

Philips says something that sounds like, "Cookies yawn hutch."

Eddy turns the water off. "What?"

"I said, cooking your lunch?"

"Oh. Yeah."

They both fall silent.

"So what are you up to today?" Philip asks.

"Nothing really. I have work tonight."

"Ah."

"It's not till later though. A few hours." Eddy twirls the cord around her finger.

"I see. Does that—I mean, are you free now?"

"Yeah."

"Can I come over? To, you know, hang out?"

Eddy hesitates only a moment. "Yeah."

Half an hour later there is a knock outside the apartment, and Eddy breathes a sigh of relief. *Good. He didn't die traveling over here.* The knock doesn't sound like it comes from the door directly, though; instead the knock is on the wall next to the door.

Eddy glances in the eyehole and opens the door. "Hi."

"Hey." Philip stands on the small porch, his camcorder still in hand. "Sorry. Your goodly charm won't even let me touch the door."

"Really? Huh. Well, it's brand-new. I guess that's why." She touches the charm and whispers the incantation that will allow the charm to recognize Philip as a friendly presence, "Ros mok-nameir."

Philip touches the goodly charm too and whispers the other half of the incantation, "Ma zahmeir."

"So, that's set. Uh, come in."

Philip smiles. "Thanks."

She pushes an unpacked box aside. "Sorry about the mess. We just moved in about two weeks ago."

"Doesn't bother me." Philip starts to raise his camcorder but stops and leaves it lowered at his side.

"So, you can have a seat. If you like. Uh, something to drink, too? I think we still have some soda." She heads toward the kitchen.

Philip plops down on the couch. "Just water's fine."

"Did it take you long to walk here?"

"No. I drove."

"Oh. Right." Eddy returns to the living area with two glasses of water. "Here." She moves to sit next to him, and Philip lifts the camcorder off the cushion first.

He accepts the water. "Thanks."

"You still have that camcorder with you?"

"Yeah. Hope you don't mind. I almost started filming when I came in." He forces a chuckle.

"I noticed." She nods and keeps her glass held up at chest level. "So, um, I don't know what to say now. Sorry. I don't normally just invite people over, you know. Don't think I do this all the time." Eddy smiles and looks away from him. *What is he going to do when he finds out I'm not a guy? How long before I have to tell him?*

"Don't worry. I only assumed the best." Philip touches her shoulder lightly.

They're both silent for a moment.

"So you've got a roommate here?"

"They're at work."

Philip looks over his shoulder. "You've got a couple living with you?"

"A couple? What—? Oh. Um, no. They—I mean, this person…um…"

"They don't prefer gendered pronouns?"

"Kinda. Yeah."

Philip nods. "I can dig it."

Eddy suddenly feels so much more relaxed around Philip. She leans back in the couch. "They're cool. Just wait until you meet them."

"Am I gonna be around long enough to meet them then?" He raises his eyebrows.

"Well, I mean, probably not today. But—"

"I mean more long term."

"Oh." Eddy bites her lower lip a moment as she raises her glass in front of her mouth. "I would hope there's a good chance of that."

They continue talking for a while. Long enough to finish their water and to end up in Eddy's room. She takes out her tarot cards and fans them out between the two of them for a moment before laying out a Celtic cross spread for Philip. He is represented by the Hanged Man and the King of Wands is crossing him. They can't decide what that part means, but in the future placement is the Wheel of Fortune, so Philip jokingly hopes he will win the lottery.

"But the Wheel is different than that," Eddy says.

"Different how?" Philip asks. They are both sitting on Eddy's bedroom floor.

"It usually means more like destiny. Let me get my notes." She reaches under her bed and pulls out an old spiral notebook with a ripped cover.

"You don't have a symbol book?"

"No. I don't need it anymore. My personal notes are better. More tailored to me." She flips through the pages and quickly finds the handwritten passage. "It can also mean a turning point—or movement more broadly speaking. As a turning point, it could reinforce the Hanged Man."

"What's this?" Philip points to a sketch of a face in the margin.

"Hm? Oh, just a little doodle."

"Are there more?"

Eddy hesitates a moment. "Yeah. In the back." She flips to the section and hands the notebook to Philip.

The sketches are of faces and whole bodies. Mostly females, some nude, some clothed. But the focus is always on the faces. The faces have the most definite lines, the most defined features.

"Did you have models?" Philip asks.

"Just reference photos from books. I wouldn't mind having a model sometime, though."

"They seem so sad. These people you've drawn."

"Yeah, I know. They're just…too full, if you know what I mean. I wish I was better at drawing. To make them more, empty, I guess. Then they could take more sadness. I remember reading somewhere that an artist should try to suck the bad out of a community through their work."

"That sounds more like what shamans were like."

"An artist can't be a shaman?" Eddy laughs.

"Not anymore. But you could be a DNA contractor."

"That definitely doesn't have the same flair."

"No. It doesn't." Philip reaches out, almost hesitantly, and touches the drawn lines with a single finger. "I don't think you should make them more empty, though."

"What do you mean?"

"Don't you know? Shamans didn't suck out sadness. They balanced it."

i will suck out the bile
in your bones
you want me to have an
answer, but I don;t have
an answer

i have no continuation,
no
/no/ no no
I want a contradiction,
becauser

you
you will leave
andyou will return and
i will notbehere,,./your
i will here,please
will

Splinter 9

Two days later, Eddy is walking home at the twilight hour. A light drizzle that had started in the morning is still falling, and Eddy is so glad she brought her umbrella to work. The walk isn't too far, and it gives her time to be alone with herself. She'd been cut early tonight due to a lack of reservations and general slow business all day. She had tried her best to stay on, but no one else wanted to go home in her place. So here she is.

Eddy touches the goodly amulet under her shirt momentarily: a habit to make sure it's always there. She steps over a puddle and approaches the apartment, worrying about the amount of money under her mattress, or rather, the lack there-of.

Inside, Eddy notices the door to Adrastos's room is closed. She holds a moment and then glances at the shoes by the door. There's an extra pair. The fuck buddy is here. She doesn't wait a moment more; she changes out of her work clothes and leaves the apartment again, trying her best to not listen for anything.

Back outside she stands on the small porch, deciding where to go. Normally she'd just go for a walk or simply be at work, which is the best solution. But now it's raining and growing dark. She goes to the apartment next door.

The people here are a younger couple, Franklin and Rosie Lesterson, only a few years older than Eddy. They have talked two or three times before. The couple even brought over cupcakes the first day she and Adrastos had moved in.

Eddy hesitates at their doorway. She assumes they're home, since the lights are on behind the window blinds, but apprehension is swirling around inside her. What if they're busy? What if they don't want company? What if they're also upset about their DNA visit that one night?

The wind picks up a moment, and the rain starts falling harder. A black shaggy strider is towering just above the tree line far off. It's trudging along slowly on its four legs, head down against the rain. Eddy sighs and decides to just knock anyway and see what happens.

A few seconds pass. The door is unlocked and opened.

Rosie opens her mouth in surprise, but that changes into a smile. "Hello! Hello. It's—it's, um…Eric, right?"

"Eddy. Actually." A smile flits up on Eddy's face, then she looks down.

"Yes, right. Eddy. Sorry. Come in, come in. Rain is picking up again." She manages the goodly charm and lets Eddy in. "Freyr really has been letting loose these last few weeks."

"Yeah. A little more than usual." Eddy puts her hands in her pockets.

This apartment has a different layout than the one she shares with Adrastos. It's one room living and dining downstairs with bedroom and bathroom upstairs. The living room itself is cozy with a couch and recliner chair in front of an entertainment case holding a large box TV and a number of different videotape players. Franklin stands up from in front of the collection, a new tape player on the floor with a tangle of cords and scattered packing peanuts from the open shipping box nearby.

"So what brings you over tonight?" Rosie asks.

"Nothing really." Eddy's eyes are still lingering on the various videotape players, thinking of Philip for a moment. "Sorry. I'm just a little displaced from the apartment right now."

"No worries," Franklin says. "I just finished installing this. Let's open a few beers. Play a board game, neighbor."

They all get settled in. Eddy finds herself tense at first, but it slowly ebbs away. They must not have been upset by that little DNA emergency incident last week. Franklin puts on a nature documentary of Yellowstone Park. The large panoramic shots and detailed close-ups of flowers were simply an excuse to highlight the enhanced detail of the new videotape format. Eddy opens and sips on a second beer. It's her turn to pull a block out of the ever more unsteady tower set up on the kitchen table.

"I just can't get over how great this new format looks." Franklin is distracted by the video again, now sitting with one arm over the back of his chair.

Eddy gently pulls out a wooden block and sets it on top of the tower. "Have you ever done any filming yourself?"

"Oh no. Not me. I'm just an appreciator."

Rosie taps her fingernail against a few blocks, testing them. "There's a fine line between appreciation and consumption."

"Huh?" Franklin turns to face her.

"Nothing, dear." She grins as she delicately rests a block high up, creating a new level. "I don't think you'll make it through your next turn."

"Ha, this is a cake walk." He starts testing blocks.

"So, I'm sure you heard about those people getting all tangled up with DNA a week ago. I heard someone was possessed, and they got quarantined."

"Uh, no, I definitely didn't hear about that part."

"Yeah, bad news all the way through. I'm just glad it wasn't me. But they were right in this building! Did you know that? I still don't know who exactly, but it's got me worried. I hope they get evicted."

"Uh, yeah." Eddy raises her beer bottle, holding it in front of her as she takes a small sip.

"What's the matter?"

"I just…don't like talking about these things."

"Who does? What if we're not safe here? What if they bring something into the whole building?"

Franklin starts pushing out a block, but the whole tower wobbles slightly. "Damn," he mutters.

Rosie laughs. "You're not even paying attention to us right now, are you?"

"Nope. Blocks." He tests another one.

"The funniest part is that you should see his brother play this game. He's a real master at it."

"That's 'cause he cheats." Finally Franklin finds a block he can remove. "He's got some latent telekinesis."

"Really? Wow. Does he work in DNA now?" Eddy asks, relieved the conversation has naturally drifted away from that goodly charm incident.

"He practically got conscripted." Franklin sets the block on top, but not carefully enough. The whole tower tips and crashes to the table, pieces flying to the floor. "Damn!"

"Looks like you lose." Rosie leans over and kisses Franklin's cheek.

Eddy helps them collect the pieces from the floor. They hadn't scattered evenly, and so Eddy ends up being the closest to the largest clump. She glances at the clock as the new tower is built; it's been a little over an hour.

Eddy steps back into the apartment, peeking down at the shoe rack. Mel's shoes are gone. Adrastos's door squeaks open, and Eddy quickly looks up. They are standing in the doorway, arms crossed, only wearing a pair of boxer briefs.

"I heard you. You left."

"You seemed busy." Eddy sits down and starts taking off her shoes. "I assume it's still you fronting, Daryl?"

"Yeah."

Neither of them say anything else as Eddy finishes and puts her shoes on the spot where Mel's had been. She walks to her room, turns the light on, and looks back at Daryl, who hasn't moved.

"What do you want?" she asks.

"I dunno. I guess I just wanted to see if you wanted to say anything."

"No. Why would I?"

"I dunno." He shrugs.

"If you really want me to say something, how about 'did you use a condom?' "

"We didn't need that."

Eddy rolls her eyes. She goes into her room and begins undressing, throwing her shirt on the floor. Daryl stands in her doorway.

"Go away. I'm gonna take a shower." Eddy enters the small walk-in closet to finish undressing.

"If you don't like him over here, I can tell him to stop coming," Daryl says.

"Really?" Eddy sticks her head out from the closet. "You'd stop cold turkey?"

"What? No. We just wouldn't do anything here."

"Yeah." Eddy disappears back into the closet. She holds her breath, keeping as silent as she can as she stands naked in the small space.

" 'Yeah,' don't bring him over again?" Daryl asks, still standing at the room's door.

"Yes. Don't bring him over again." Eddy comes out wearing a bathrobe, tying the cords around her waist.

Daryl just nods and steps aside, letting her pass into the bathroom.

i have no more

words you see. II cant in anyway

go home,, home is not here. IT is no where
nowhere for you.
My Eyes have been set ablaize with
shadowsand heat. My Eyes coudln,t see eeee
even if they wanted to see. You. You
do hold something, but it is not what he
thinks or expects. IT is not for him to
evereverevereverevereverevereverevereverebe
ever see. Never truly though. Never truly
know.

Be atlarge. No. Be at pease. These ghosts
ssss will no longer haunt you. Not now.
                    but perhaps again.
Our circle is discontinuious, Painfully
so. Painfully un.   unwell
      My shadowed mirror holds no salva-
tion.
      Do you see yet? Now? Bwfore?
Perhaps next time when the rains have dispe
and the clouds are still as ever dark as
befobe . . . ll. . ...

and all
       the rests is
                   just
                       bla nkness.

Splinter 10

"Why do cockroaches always end up on their back when they die?" Noah asks. "Doesn't that take more effort? You know, since they're so flat, I'm sure it's really hard to roll over."

Eddy sits at the kitchen table, sipping tea as she doodles. She's wearing just a sweater and underwear. Sleep had been difficult last night, and so she ended up awake much earlier than normal. Noah is squatting by the cupboard under the sink, poking at a dying roach as he waits for his toast to finish cooking. He has work this morning.

He yawns. "Wouldn't it just be easier for them to fall on their stomachs if they're dying of poison? That would make so much more sense."

Eddy sighs. It's difficult to look at Noah, to see the same body as Daryl just the night before. "I guess." She closes her eyes and rests her head on the table, over her doodles. She's not looking forward to today.

"How do roaches even work?" He smiles and glances up at Eddy.

She rolls her pen back and forth on the table.

Noah's smile slowly fades as she doesn't respond. The toast dings and pops up.

He collects the toast, looking down, and mumbles the answer, "We just don't know."

She should apologize. She should say something. But the effort, the effort involved in that and the effort she needs to save.

"Sorry. Tired," is all she manages.

Noah slathers margarine over the toast and sits down next to Eddy. He bumps her shoulder with his forehead. "Feel better."

Eddy gives a momentary closed-mouth smile. "Thanks."

Noah takes a small bite, the bread crunching beneath his teeth. "Um, the thing is coming today right? The people? DNA?"

"Yeah." She sits up. "Probably in an hour. After you've left."

Noah continues eating, not speaking again until he starts on the second piece. "It—it could be nothing, you know? Could just be us. Us being too worried."

Eddy starts tracing a vajra on the back of her hand to help her focus. "I guess we'll see."

Eddy dresses. Then she continues doodling as she waits, using the flowing pen strokes to keep herself from thinking about what is fast approaching, using them to stem her anxiety. A knock comes from the door.

She looks up and bites her bottom lip. Alright, this is it. Time to get whatever this is all squared away. Eddy stands, hesitates at the door, and opens it.

A man wearing a tan work jumpsuit with the DNA logo embroidered on the breast pocket is standing on their excuse for a porch. He holds a clipboard and has a rolling cart behind him.

"Eduardo Caller? I'm Michael Hawthorn with the Department of Nonhuman Affairs. Ex-druid, though that bit's not part of the official spiel here. In fact, that time is all wrapped up nice and tidy and tossed in the river, but you don't care about that part. I've got paper work for you."

"Oh. I've, uh, yeah. Heard about those older things. Um."—she reaches over and rubs an elbow—"I actually prefer Eddy. Not—not Eduardo."

"Fine. *Eddy* Caller. I've got your address here, filed with a 'request for rediagnosis,' case number is seventy-eight forty-eight dash B. Symptoms being general anxiety, possible memory loss, and possible exposer." Hawthorn speaks in a slightly droning manner, hardly even looking at her while reading off the information. "Here's the verification papers. Just need your signature." He holds the clipboard up.

"Uh." Eddy looks at the paper work before her, not knowing what any of it means. "Uh, this—this is being covered by our apartment complex. Right?"

The man rolls his eyes. "Yeah, you're set. Everything regarding the apartment will be billed to management. Now can I get this started?" He lifts the clipboard a little higher.

"Sure. Here. Let me, um, here." She touches the goodly charm to let him in. "Ros mok-nameir."

"Ma zahmär," Hawthorn pronounces crisply. He steps inside the apartment and hands the clipboard to Eddy directly. "I'll start setting up this equipment. Most of the readings will be done today, but some will take a few days to get a proper gauge." He pulls the cart in as well. "All the doors unlocked in here?"

"Yeah." Eddy is looking at the paper work on the clipboard, still hesitant to sign.

Hawthorn starts unpacking the cart, laying out a number of devices and a tripod on the couch. He glances over at Eddy. "You have to sign if you want me to get to work on this. I do have other appointments today."

"Sorry," Eddy says quietly. She scribbles her signature and 4/28/92 at the bottom of the sheet and hands it back over.

Hawthorn tucks it into an outer pouch on the cart. "It'll take me just a bit to set all this up. Going to put some thermometers around, have to set up this EVP recorder, take a few readings." Hawthorn begins extending a tripod and connecting a large, fuzzy microphone to the top. "This records audio and the electronic voice phenomena, blah blah. You've probably heard of this before. And I know you won't want it recording all the time so just switch it on around midnight or whenever you go to sleep. There's a tape already loaded. Just push this button." He points to a button on top of the recorder.

"Me?"

"Yes. I won't be here longer than an hour." Hawthorn withdraws a number of blank pages from a manila envelope. He also collects a handful of small circular thermometers with adhesive backs. Hawthorn sticks one page and one thermometer to the wall in the living area.

"Why is that page blank?"

He glances over his shoulder. "These are pages of 'anomalous paper.' They've got some metaphysical properties, just like the Alduer Ljósemannt. You won't need to worry about them while they're hung up here." He proceeds into the kitchen and the bedrooms.

Eddy stands awkwardly near the couch, feeling displaced in her own home. Her first thought is to go get her tarot cards, but she worries she might look inept in the eyes of a real druid, ex or not. She rubs the back of her left hand, smearing the vajra without realizing it.

Hawthorn returns to the living room and drops the extra thermometers into the cart. "I'm not going to bother with the photo sweep today." He puts an instant camera back into the cart. "I'll do a quick ion and EMF sweep. Then we'll get to the real diagnosis." Hawthorn takes two handheld devices and again tours the apartment. Each device has a small screen with numbers displayed.

After a minute or two Hawthorn returns. "Nothing out of the ordinary." He jots down a few notes. "I don't even know why checking all these things is the new set-in-stone policy. They almost never turn up anything we don't already know." He stuffs the ion and EMF meters into the cart and pulls out a new device. "This though, this is the real deal here. This is a real tool."

This new item looks rather simple—a rectangle, about the size of a remote, with a dial on the front near the bottom and a number of small LEDs along the side. In the center is a plastic window revealing a clear quartz crystal within.

"This is an MVM, a metaphysical vibration meter. This thing detects even minute vibrations in the quartz crystal and shows their strength. But only plebeians use this crude casing." He starts popping off the cover. "People not classically trained. People who wouldn't even be able to tell if the crystal was upside down or not." Hawthorn finally frees the crystal from the meter and tosses the casing on the couch. He holds both points of the quartz between his thumb and index finger. "Don't tell anyone I'm doing this. It's not up to the new code, but these old ways are far superior."

"Uh… okay."

Hawthorn closes his eyes and starts walking very slowly through the apartment. He avoids everything, though—stepping over the last of the boxes, moving around furniture, holding his hand out to push doors aside—never opening his eyes. Eddy tilts her head to the side in wonder. Had he memorized these locations? Or was he "seeing" them right now?

After almost fifteen minutes, Hawthorn finally makes his way back into the main room, walking right up to Eddy. He raises his hand, holding the crystal directly in front of Eddy's forehead, and Hawthorn's eyebrows furrow over his still-closed eyes.

"Uh." Eddy blinks and steps back.

Hawthorn steps forward in synch with her.

"Mr. H-Hawthorn?"

He opens his eyes. "Nothing's here."

Eddy waits a moment, expecting him to say something more.

Hawthorn rubs his forehead with his free hand, dropping his other hand to his side. "I'm not detecting anything. I've dealt with almost everything this part of the continent can throw at a person, and I can't find a scrap of anything. But…" He nods toward Adrastos's room. "What's your roommate?"

"Wha—what do you mean?"

"I think you know what I mean. I'm getting mental traces of several people, six in total. Some more frequent than others, but I'd wager at least two nonhumans and something else very, very old." Hawthorn crosses his arms. "Do you know about this?"

Eddy looks down at the ground. "It's not them."

"I know."

She glances up. "They're a system. That's it. Just a normal system."

Hawthorn nods. "Right. Systems are easy to throw under the bus. I'll leave them out of my report." He picks up the husk of the MVM and puts the quartz crystal back. "By the way, have you even taken a Seidr Five-Point test?"

"Uh, no."

"Perhaps you should sometime. But I'll pack up now. Don't forget that audio recorder these next few nights. I doubt it'll glean any useful evidence, though. I didn't detect anything, so there's nothing here now."

"But, what about the, you know, the things. The things we've been feeling."

"There are no things you've been feeling. You filled out the forms yourself, and you didn't list a single symptom. The only thing we have to go on are your four memory lapses, and those aren't terribly uncommon." He repacks the cart and zips it up. "I'll be back in a week to pick up the equipment. We'll call to give you a heads-up. If there really is anything, we'll know by then."

V

Tomorrow I shall awake n from
frozen waters and stride through
hallways, corridoors.

I will go to
no place and you will still try
and follow. /why/ Why?

yOU might think to know or need, but You
don't want what I have been given here...
Hear. Sight will fail and only ears will
have a hope of finding. Falling.
Grasped under and held, nothing, suck in
and like fountain expire, exhail.

Exumed
before the ghosts
could lay claim to
to the present as well.

why do you try, thigns you don;y
understand. He will claim you re-
gaurdless. Like roots dug into
soil and churred up like butter or
froth.

The entirety of your being
will be stewed up and drowned
in expectations. Like juggling
inside your organs, yo[illegible] s

Dear me I can[illegible]
anymore, s[illegible]
and get [illegible]

Splinter 11

Eddy doesn't know what to do with the rest of her day. She doesn't have work, and Adrastos won't be back for hours. She paces around the apartment, still upset and worried about the initial diagnosis Hawthorn had given her. The thermometers and anomalous paper are hung in every room, even the bathrooms, not allowing Eddy to displace the thoughts of DNA from her mind.

She peeks into Adrastos's room and sees the two items hanging on the wall there as well. Eddy crosses her arms tightly around herself, hugging her sides with her hands. She paces back through the apartment and eventually returns to her room.

Time passes by at a mercilessly slow pace. The anxiety will not melt away. Eddy grabs her tarot deck, crawls into bed, and curls up in a ball under the covers. She just clutches her abuela's cards, not using them. She feels so cold and shivers as a headache creeps into her brain. Desperately she wishes none of this would continue; she wishes none of this would come to anything. What can she possibly do?

The sky outside slowly darkens, and Eddy uncoils, eventually able to steady herself enough to read in short spurts. She glances at the clock.

Eight forty-four. That late already? Where is Adrastos? Why aren't they back yet? *What if they died? Got hit by a car while walking home?*

Eddy sits up slowly. Only her desk lamp is on. She stands, approaches the switch for the ceiling light, and half raises her hand. She stands there. Legs slightly apart, eyes fixed on the light switch, hand suspended in the air, fingers slightly outstretched.

She doesn't move.

She's fairly calm, thinking about the next few steps in her course of action. *Adrastos isn't back yet. Maybe they just stopped somewhere. Maybe the fuck buddy's place. I hope not. I'm not going to turn the light on yet. Where else might they go? The library? Noah had mentioned something about a usenet group. Something on the Internet I don't understand. I'm choosing not to finish raising my hand. I just need to think a minute. I've been on the Internet like twice. Noah is the only person I know who has any proficiency with it. Why aren't I turning the light on? I guess I'm just seeing how long I can hold this pose. I can move if I want. I'm just pretending. I can move.*

Eddy opens her mouth slightly, thinking she will lick her lips, but she doesn't. She rolls her eyes to look at her hand in front of her, then back to the light switch. She has a thought that she is actually a bit comfortable right now.

Just turn on the light switch. Just turn on the light switch. I'll do it in a minute. Just need a minute. I guess I'll go to the library. A nice walk will help me feel better. Why won't I turn on the light switch? Why?

Eddy feels her pulse start to quicken. Why is she pretending she can't move? She just doesn't know. This is such a silly thing to do. She has to go. She has to turn on the light. Slowly, with focus, she twitches her fingers. Yes. She stares at her hand, only concentrating on the slight twitching at the tips of her extremities. Eddy twitches her wrist next, rotating it ever so slowly.

See? I'm doing this. I'm just pretending. Move. Move!

She keeps twitching her fingers and wrist as much as she can, which is only the slightest of movement. Finally, finally she jitters her whole forearm to the elbow, curling it up slightly, and then she's free. She stops pretending. She brings her feet together and drops her arm with a sigh.

That was stupid. Why was I pretending like that?

Eddy shakes her head and turns on the light.

Half an hour later Eddy is walking down the sidewalk, the road only illuminated by streetlights. There's no one nearby: no people walking, no cars passing. A slight drizzle is falling over the world, the drops not large enough to make any sound. Everything around her is as silent as a crowded elevator.

The library isn't far away. Eddy fiddles with her amulet through the fabric of her shirt, glancing side to side every few minutes. She turns a corner and sees the building now: the parking lot mostly empty with several streetlamps illuminating the area, the light twinkling gently off the damp asphalt.

Eddy doesn't know how late the library is open. She's never tried tracking Adrastos down before when they've been away. She stops in the middle of the parking lot, considering. She takes a step back and almost turns around, but doesn't look away from the double glass doors. There's no point in leaving; she's already here.

Inside seems even quieter than outside. The entry area has a higher ceiling than the rest of the building and tiled floor instead of carpeting where the bookshelves are. No one is at the checkout desk, but a small sign set on the counter reads: "Attendant will return shortly."

Are they already closed? Eddy doesn't see anyone anywhere, but the doors hadn't been locked. She tiptoes across the tile, not wanting to break the silence. On the carpet, among the books, the shelves loom over her, almost touching the lower ceiling. If Eddy reaches up, the tips of her fingers can touch the white squares above her head. There clearly aren't enough shelves in the building: each one is jam-packed, every space filled, impossible to see beyond to the row just next door. The computers are somewhere back here. Past the shelves. The carpet keeps Eddy's footsteps muffled, hidden. She reaches a T in the bookshelves and turns, seeing more shelves. Where is she?

Eddy looks over her shoulder in the other direction. More books. More shelves. She keeps walking, now looking for the edge of the building, anything to help guide her.

Another turn, another row. The light above this aisle is flickering slowly, a soft strobe: dim, then bright, then dim again.

At the end of the flickering aisle, the cap on the shelf says Eddy is at nonfiction 910–919. She's nearly at the end then. Nearly out. One last corner and she sees them.

Eight computers all in a row against the wall. The lights overhead are less bright here. Every one of the box monitors is off except one, silhouetting a head facing the screen. Their shoulder bag is laid out on the floor beside their chair, and Eddy steps forward silently, a small grin forming on her lips.

She clasps her hands over their eyes. "Guess who!"

"Ah!" They scream out once, jumping in their seat and frantically grasping at the fingers that cover their face, fingernails scratching into skin.

"Ay! Aguas!" Eddy pulls away and covers the back of her left hand. "What was that for?"

They turn around, his features obscured by the light all around their face. "Oh, Eddy! What the hell did *you* do that for? I thought I was about to get murdered."

"I was just trying to prank you. Geez." She checks her hand. It's bleeding, but not much.

"Sorry," he says softly. "I panicked."

Eddy knows it's Noah speaking to her now. She pulls out the chair next to him and sits down, still putting pressure on the scratch. "It's okay. I guess I asked for this."

Noah tilts his head to one side, raising that shoulder as well in a sort of nod shrug. "You—you gonna be okay?"

"Yeah."

"Okay." Noah turns back to the computer screen and begins typing again.

Eddy watches him for a few moments and then leans back in the chair and looks around at the other machines. "How did they afford all of these here? I though these new things were expensive."

"A donor, I think. There's a plaque somewhere around here. The Trammels, slash the Timbersons, slash, or maybe both. I dunno."

"Oh." Eddy checks her hand again.

For several minutes they're both silent as Noah continues typing away. He yawns, comes to a stopping point, and looks over at Eddy. "Why are you here?"

"I dunno." She pauses. "You were late. I guess, I just thought I'd come look for you. You know." *I didn't want to be alone.*

"Here is where I am. Just doing my thing." He looks back at the box monitor.

Eddy leans over, looking at the screen as well. It's just a lot of text in a large gray box with a few other gray boxes and some icons at the top. "How do you understand all this?"

"It's easy," Noah says without looking away from the screen. "Rudimentary even. Where I came from there was a lot more of this, and even better. Way better." He raises his head slightly, his face blank for a moment. He glances at Eddy. "Like me. I think." His eyebrows press together as his eyes drift away from her. He licks his lips and blinks a few times before returning to the screen.

Eddy smiles a little and pushes his shoulder lightly. "You're so spacey sometimes."

"I guess."

She leans in again. "What's that? 'startarus42?' "

"My handle," Noah answers.

"A what?"

"User name. You know. What I go by."

"Oh."

A little more times passes. The scratch on Eddy's hand stops bleeding. Noah remains focused on the computer as Eddy begins to wonder why she did come here. She sighs. Noah is too distracted to notice, and he yawns again.

Shortly, an older man walks by and lets them know the library is closing in ten minutes. Noah finishes up and collects his bag, and the two of them leave. Noah guides Eddy through the bookcases. He knows them by heart.

Outside, in the dark and silence, Noah says, "It's nice you're here, though. Don't have to walk home alone."

"What about the others?"

"It's not the same as you being here."

They walk home without talking. Home is where the DNA equipment is. Eddy definitely doesn't want to talk about that. About halfway there Noah stops.

"What is it?" Eddy asks.

"One of the people in my usenet group pointed out something insightful today."

"What?"

"That we're all wounded. From the moment we're born and come screaming into life, this world scars us." Noah looks over at her. "And do you know what those scars are called?"

"Uh…" Eddy swallows. "Can we, not talk about this?"

Noah half smiles and says softly, "Bellybuttons. They're bellybuttons."

Eddy doesn't reply for a few seconds. "Let's just get home."

He looks down at the sidewalk. "Okay."

You think you can see me yet
but you can;t see me yet, can;t
recult my twisting heart and I
am a [illegible] in these shafows here
, cloud cast covers
here.

My
iyes
will never
be like yours
that
always try
to /u/ seek
after

Splinter 12

A few days later Eddy finally gets to see Philip again. Before he comes over, Eddy takes down all the thermometers and anomalous paper, hiding them and the EVP equipment in Adrastos's closet.

Admitting they have DNA investigating their house would be the same as admitting you had warts all over your toes, or reoccurring exceptionally loud bowel movements that were the wrong color. This is only the third time she's seeing Philip. She doesn't want him to know anything about DNA at all.

Once he's here, at the apartment—safe from the travel—and they've gotten to the point where momentum is moving on its own accord and the talking, the interacting, no longer have that awkward film sticking over it, Eddy relaxes. She forgets about DNA.

They're sitting on the floor in her room, their backs against her bed. Eddy has just finishing showing Philip one of her old sketch books that's completely full. His camera sits unused on her desk.

"So now it's your turn." Eddy smiles. "Tell me something about you that you don't share with anyone."

"Ah, that's so hard now that I'm on the spot." Philip throws his head back a moment. "I dunno. If we were in my room this would be a lot easier."

"Really?"

"I mean because I'd have my things around. I'd have some material to work with."

"Mm-hmm. Well. What about your camera?" Eddy points to it.

"What about it?"

"Why do you always carry it around?"

"I already told you that." Philip crosses his arms. "I've carried it around since high school. I love filming. Maybe I'll make a movie one day."

"And that's it?"

Philip is silent. After a few seconds Eddy starts to worry she somehow made him upset.

"I'm sorry," she says quickly.

"For what?"

"Uh, pushing you, I guess. I dunno. You got all quiet."

Philip sucks his lips in for a moment, then looks at her. "Sorry. I just—it's just…high school wasn't, great."

Eddy forces a laugh. "I don't know anyone who liked high school."

"That doesn't surprise me," he says quietly. "For us, it's—it's so much harder. You know what I mean."

"Uh…" What does he mean?

Philip leans toward her a little. "Liking guys."

"Oh. Right. Yeah. That." She bites her lower lip and looks away. That was half of it. Oh no. He only likes guys. But she's not actually a guy.

"I mean, I thought—don't you?" Philip asks. "Aren't you…?"

She should say it. She should say it right now: I don't identify as a guy, but damn, you are so attractive. My body is a guy, but if I could wish myself to match my mind, I'd be a girl. But you like boys…

"Y-yeah. Sorry. I, uh, don't normally talk about it." She hesitates a moment, then adds more quietly, "Liking guys."

"You're not out?"

"No. Not to anyone here but my roommate."

"Are you two…?"

"No," Eddy says quickly.

Philip nods. "Okay. Yeah, sorry. That was kinda awkward." He looks away.

Eddy thought they had gotten past that today. Dammit. What can she do? A coldness comes over her body and she shivers a moment. Touch. Just, don't, be, alone.

She puts a hand on Philip's knee.

He looks back at her with a small smile and puts his hand over hers. "Being black also doesn't help."

"I can imagine."

"It's probably worse than you imagine. It's so hard to know things without living them. And being black and liking guys, that's really hard. The black community they…it's just really frowned on. It all gets squeezed out. Like being suffocated."

"Like being crushed."

Philip nods.

Eddy is silent a moment, just looking at Philip's hand on hers. She's feeling warmer inside as her heart starts to beat stronger. She forces a laugh. "Sorry. I asked about your camcorder and now we're talking about this."

"It kind of relates, actually." Philip starts rubbing the back of Eddy's hand with his thumb. "You see, high school was bad. I got picked on a lot. Sometimes really bad. You know, just dark days back then. But my uncle, he helped me a lot. Back when I didn't know anything. Didn't know how to handle anything. We were always really close, but high school was when he helped me the most."

"What did he do? I mean, if that's okay to ask."

"He sent me that camcorder. Well, it's complicated. He wasn't actually there anymore. Not then. He, well, my mother and him had a falling out. I dunno over what. He was on my dad's side, so I dunno, I guess they never got along. But she forbade me from ever seeing him again when I was thirteen. I used to hang out with him all the time when my mom was at work, usually over the summer when school was out. He didn't live far from my house. He would pick me up, and we'd spend the whole day in the woods on his property. Taught me about making fires and how to use an axe, all kinds of things. I guess it was kind of dangerous, but it was just like being in Boy Scouts, right? I never was one, so I dunno for sure."

"Me either," Eddy says. "Sounds like it, though."

Philip nods. "But when he sent me that camcorder, it was like my saving grace. I started taking film classes, and I always had it with me for school, so that's when I started carrying it everywhere. But it was more than that. More than just a video recorder." He hesitates. "It was like my shield, in a way. If they were coming toward me, I could pull it up, start filming those guys, and they wouldn't bother me. They knew they couldn't because I'd have proof. I started doing it all the time."

"That's…that's neat. Like, really. That sounds like a really good idea."

Philip scoots a little closer to Eddy, their shoulders touching. "It's how I got through high school."

Eddy doesn't reply. She's too focus on his body next to hers. She's in disbelief. Out of all the people at the DNA branch that morning, she met this person. This person who's actually interested in her. In her as a person. She hopes.

"What about you?" he asks. "What was your high school like?"

"Nothing really. I mean, nothing. Nothing to talk about. But you know, I'm really glad that camcorder helped you so much. If not, I mean, you might not be here."

"Let's not get too fatalistic."

"I mean, you know it. It's so—so easy to be crushed by people. Everything will seem so fine and normal one day, then the next they're devouring you. Mercilessly." Eddy hesitates. "I do have one story from high school."

"What?"

"It's not even my story. It really kills me, though—these things, when they happen. When the group of others, the group you once were part of, start thinking they're so right. My father moved me here to this state when I was twelve, but not this city. We lived in the city on the state border south of here. That's where I went to high school. I met Adrastos there."

"Who?"

"Uh. I mean Glen."

"Your roommate? Is his last name Adrastos? Isn't that Greek?"

"No, sorry. That's a…it's like a nickname. Long story to it. Anyways, I was part of this one circle of people. Friends with several of them. But there was this other guy, Ross. He was on the other side of the circle, so I didn't hang out with him unless we were all together. I don't even know the whole story, but the other side of the circle went to this convention one time, and I dunno, they just broke. Completely. Ross got ejected from the group. No one, no one at all associated with him again. There was some fight or disagreement on the trip that escalated, and then everyone else started hating him. Everything he did from then on was bad, and they turned him into this monster almost. He lost most of the people he called friends.

"Something like that happened in college, too, but worse. I only went two years, and I hung out with this group of people a lot there. There were these two guys who were dating, and they had this apartment that was like our hub, and, well, that's a different story. But that's how I met all my college friends.

"There was this one guy though, Nick, and he hung out with us, too. But he was also on the other side of the circle, not directly my friend. He was only around for a few months before it happened. People just started hating him, and I don't even know why. The only explanation I ever got was that he was annoying. That he argued too much. And they threw him out. Just like that. Gone. And he was a freshman too, from out of state, so he hardly knew anyone besides our group.

"I saw him around campus a few times after that but never talked to him. Eventually I saw him with a new group of people, so I guess he found better friends, so it turned out alright, I guess. But I don't understand why that had to happen to him.

"And there's a last one. More recent, from my last job, this other restaurant I worked at. It was such a toxic place. No one cared. It's really good that I got away from it, but there was a server there, Matt, who got promoted to team leader when I was there. And he was really good at it. He actually cared. He actually wanted to do his job as well as he could. But no one helped him. No one respected him. The managers didn't even give him the training he was supposed to get. I heard him talking about it once to his girlfriend, how he got this corporate team leader book with all the information in it, and the managers were supposed to go over the whole thing with him one-on-one. But they never did. No one cared.

"Eventually he stepped down. Became a normal server again. He just couldn't take it. And that's when they destroyed him. They stopped giving him good shifts. When he was there, he didn't get as many tables as the rest of us. He wasn't making enough money, and he left. He had to. And it was horrible. I—I really respected him. But I never told him. We weren't on that level with each other, but I wish I had told him. So he could have known that at least one person believed in him. I dunno." Eddy shakes her head and looks at the floor. "I guess I've just always been afraid that something like that would happen to me, because it always happens so randomly. Without warning. How were any of them supposed to know?"

Philip is silent for a while after Eddy's story. He simply slides his hand across the back of hers, interlink their fingers. Finally he asks, "Are you always on the outside?"

"Huh?"

"You never knew any of these people directly."

"Oh." Eddy had never realized that element. "No. I—I didn't. That's just how it happened, I guess."

Philip is silent a moment more. "I think a more specific question is, has anything happened to you?"

"What? Me?" Eddy blinks. "No. Nothing bad has ever happened to me. I just see it. Sometimes."

Philip nods. "Well, you're lucky then. It does seem to be the way the world works. The ones who aren't homogenous are the ones who get trampled."

"Yeah." Eddy wants to say something else, but she isn't sure if she should. But she does. "I mean, there's…uh, even Glen. Even my roommate has a horrible story. His parents died to the Bad News our last year of high school. They were downtown when they heard it. Laid themselves out in the street, and the bus driver didn't see them in time."

"Really? But, I thought it was contained."

"Mostly contained. I know DNA has it as a top priority, but even if just one person writes it down before suiciding, then the whole things starts again. What can you do against something that's not physical?"

The apartment door opens and closes. Eddy's own door is only open a crack, so they don't see anyone.

"That's my roommate now."

"I assume he knows?" Philip raises their linked hands slightly.

"Yeah. It's fine. My roommate's cool."

They sit in silence for several seconds. A slight ringing begins to fill Eddy's ears, but then Philip speaks.

"Do you think DNA will ever save the world? Make it actually a safe place?"

"They say they can. But they're just a government department. I dunno." Eddy suddenly wants to know why Philip had been in that DNA branch. What had he needed? What is he dealing with? Is *he* safe?

She doesn't ask.

"It'd be nice," Philip says softly. He squeezes her hand a little. "Just think. Getting to swim in the ocean. Commercial air travel. And their public campaign is totally focused on finally being able to cut down the Forest of Knives in the Midwest."

"You're into all that political stuff?"

"Just what I hear on the radio." He chuckles.

Eddy smiles a moment and stands. "I'm gonna get some water. Do you want some?"

"Sure." Philip stretches out his arms. "No ice, please."

"You got it."

Eddy opens her door only enough to slip out and lets it swing shut behind her. The rest of the apartment is still dark, not a single light is on. Hadn't Adrastos gotten home like eight minutes ago?

Eddy flips on the kitchen light and grabs two glasses, filling them with water from the tap. She turns around and sees Adrastos. Just standing there. In the middle of the living room, partially illuminated from the light spilling out of the kitchen. Their face is impassive, and their arms hang loosely at their side.

Mother , Matron , and Crown. IN dead tr
ee
tree caskets firmented, frestered, cured,
?? you say?/
no. // this isn;y a way to t
he place above set. set for you
You.
in hasal
llowed hells befor beyond. yuo castastrayed
people. people. me.

for what

idon,t have ahrest for holding. my blood

is like sap, aged, flowing, notflowing
dripping
Suckled by damp mosses, holy. hallowed
What /more / canyou claim??
//
what more can I? ??
I led you.
feed. fed
you
bled
our Anthem is fadingout like a slowing YOU
record.
whit scratches inbetween
these lines
.

Splinter 13

"Adrastos?" Eddy asks quietly. "What's up? What are you doing?"

They don't reply. They just stand there, staring forward at nothing.

Eddy sets the glasses of water down. What's happening? Why is this happening *now*? Philip is right here, right in the other room, and this—whatever it is—is happening.

Eddy takes a few steps toward them, keeping her voice low. "Adrastos? Adrastos." She pokes their chest.

"Who?" they ask softly.

"What?" Dammit, why is this happening! What can she do? Eddy frets a moment, but then a silly idea comes to mind. She takes Adrastos by the shoulders and flops them down on the couch.

They don't resist. They simply lie there, slightly askew, staring up at the ceiling.

Eddy goes back to her room, opening the door only enough for her to slip in.

"What's up?" Philip asks, still sitting on the floor.

"Um. They, um, Glen said he isn't feeling good. He's, he's lying down. I think you'll have to…go. Sorry." She bites her lip.

"Oh. Oh, that's okay." He pushes himself up from the floor and takes his camcorder.

Eddy leads him to the front door, glancing at Adrastos as she goes. She doesn't stop until both she and Philip are standing on the tiny porch outside with the door closed, blocking them off from the inside.

"Sorry to cut this off so suddenly," Eddy says softly.

Philip shakes his head. "It's okay." He pauses. "You'll call me? When you're free again?"

"Yes. Definitely. I'll call you tomorrow." Eddy takes a half step back, her fingers touching the doorknob.

Philip leans forward and kisses her, catching her on the lips. Just one small kiss.

Eddy's breath hangs up a moment: a slight inhale expanding her chest, locking it there. It's like drowning in cement.

Philip has a slight smile on his face, but it quickly slips away. He opens his mouth slightly, hesitates, and asks, "Are…was that, too quick?"

Her lungs finally release in a tiny exhale. Was that really it? That small amount of air was keeping her body frozen? "No. No, I'm sorry. I'll call you." She retreats into the apartment, not looking back.

Adrastos is no longer on the couch.

Eddy stands with her back against the door, eyes shut, holding her breath. She thinks she can hear Philip's footsteps walking away. "Dammit. *Dammit*," she says with a splintering voice. She sucks in a deep breath and looks up. "Adrastos! What the shit is happening to you?"

There's no reply. There's only a *tack, tack, tacking* streaming from their room, the drops of sound halting then rushing.

Ding.

She approaches their room, the heel of her palm rubbing her right eye.

Bzzzpt.

They are there, hunched over the typewriter once gifted to them by their biogrands, fingers fumbling furiously over the keys, the sheet of paper more than half spent. *Tack tack tack—klack*! Two of the small metal type arms clash together and stick, but this has no effect on Adrastos. They keep floundering over the keys as if they're doggy-paddling through water.

"Adrastos!" Eddy grabs their shoulder and swivels both them and the chair away from the typewriter.

They slump slightly into the pull, listing sideways. Their head rolls back, mouth agape loosely, and look up at Eddy. "Here."

"What?"

"Here."

Eddy is still holding them by the shoulder, but now she leans back. Adrastos lists farther sideways and lets themselves fall to the floor with a slight *thump*, spilled out across the carpet.

Eddy hops back, a reflexive action. She quickly crouches down and touches their chest. "What is wrong with you? Are you okay?" She has never seen them act like this before. Should she tell DNA about this?

"Here. Here is different." They roll over, away from Eddy. "Need grasping. Sky is different. Trees are different. Grass different. Need to not be here." They push themselves up and stumble toward the door, but their feet miss the proper steps, and they careen off course, running into the wall.

"Gods." Eddy gets up and grabs one of their arms, keeping them from leaving the room.

Adrastos flatten themselves front forward against the surface. With their free hand, they spread their fingers across the wall, flexing the joints as if they could dive their fingers into the plaster and scoop out a chunk. "Here," they say again, their voice faltering.

Eddy has to do something. The only likely scenarios she can imagine are that they've been possessed somehow or that they've gained a new member to the system who has no idea what's happening. She pulls them away from the wall and reaches up to their chest, pressing her hand against their body to check if they have their goodly amulet on. Eddy doesn't feel it at first and starts sliding her hand from one side to the other, searching in case it's been caught somewhere in the fabric.

But they jerk away, slipping their arm from her gasp. They run from the room.

Eddy is off balance a moment from their sudden escape, but she dashes after them.

you dont, i know, know yet
eye
its me, mine, over spun simply
across, around, far.
her determination is
riddled through TV
screens, static screams,
static/crawl//static
alone. boister. bound.
his followers to exodus
ten, to house pooling,
house sermons, h

if for nothing more, eye
TV lines
static lines
/

Splinter 14

Adrastos is already out the door by the time Eddy makes it into the main room. She hesitates at the threshold to the outside world. A light rain is falling, and it's night. It's dark. Dangerous.

But she has to. She has to get Adrastos. They might not have their goodly amulet on. They will die. Death will finally come stamping its feet around her, and she is frozen, watching the fading image of Adrastos's white sweatshirt across the apartment complex.

"No," she moans, her voice almost nonexistent. "Please, no." She takes a step outside. Closes the door. "Anubis preserve me."

Eddy sets off running.

Adrastos is not taking the sidewalks or the streets or the normal pathways. They are running off the regularly trawled places, running to the fence, over it, into the woods.

"Adrastos!" Eddy screams out as they disappear among the trees.

She reaches the fence faster than her thoughts and fears can keep up. With a quick heave and kicking of her legs to gain traction, she gets one foot over the fence and drops down. The twisted metal at the top catches her other leg and tears the cuff of her jeans, biting into her skin just above the ankle.

"Ay! Dammit. Shit." Eddy staggers a moment and looks down. The jeans aren't ripped more than a few inches, but the blood is visible on her white socks. This is too dangerous. Things will smell her blood. Things in the night and in the forest.

She looks up into the deep blackness of the gathered trees and sees no sign of Adrastos. Adrastos.

"*Dammit.*" Eddy runs. Runs faster than before, ignoring the rain. Through the trees and across muddy earth that starts sucking at her feet, squelching and slopping and slowing her too much. She can't see her feet. Can hardly see even a few inches before her, like swimming through ink. Several times she collides with a tree or trips over the underbrush. She's not even sure she's heading in the same direction.

By providence or good fortune, the clouds overhead begin to thin—letting some small starlight trickle down into the forest. But there is still so much mud, too much mud. The puddles keep growing deeper as she is swallowed farther into the forest. Fungus and moss are growing on the trees, great caps inches in diameter cluster around the roots, being trampled under her feet.

Far ahead of her, where the trees seem at least somewhat sparser, Eddy catches a quick splash of white from Adrastos's sweatshirt. She races toward it with renewed vigor, the skin across her body crawling and her head now pounding with a sudden ache. Something is right behind her, she knows it, she knows it. Something with cracked antlers and teeth and blood dripping from its mouth mixed with spit and bile—its stomach ruptured across fur from gorging itself after years and decades and centuries—it will skewer her across its foot-long claws and chew off her skin and suck out her eyes. She knows it. Eddy tucks her head down and ignores the tears on her face as she forces her legs to run, run, paddling against the mud and skipping over roots that keep coming like waves. And she is free.

The forest ends, and she falls to her knees outside on the open grassy field, panting. Everything below her waist is covered with mud. There's leaves in her hair and wet grass sticking to her fingers. She does not look back.

As she raises her head she sees a road, and across from it is the library's parking lot. How is that possible? The library is farther away than that. Even running, how had she gotten here so quick? Now she glances back. Just forest. Just trees. The rain has stopped, and the streetlights are on, and nothing is here at all besides the empty concrete cradle, and Adrastos standing in the middle of it.

Eddy pushes herself up, leaving mud tracks across the grass and road as she joins her roommate in the parking lot.

"Adrastos! What are you doing?"

They don't respond. Adrastos is standing on a raised island in the parking lot with grass and a few trees. They have their back to her, looking up at the sky, arms spread out slightly.

Eddy approaches them slowly, but before she can reach them, Adrastos turns around. There are about four yards between them.

"Have you, ever noticed?" they ask. "Even after the rain stops…it keeps falling from the trees?"

"What are you talking about?"

"Here. Look." They raise their hand, pointing at the small decorative trees and the canopy of branches above.

Water is still falling from the leaves, rain deferred. Eddy wonders a moment: if there were enough trees on the whole planet, might it rain forever?

"Who—who am I talking to?" she asks.

"Me?" Adrastos's eyes go unfocused and slide away. "I don't have a name for you to forsake."

"What? Then who are you?"

Adrastos is silent for almost a minute. "No one…" He drags out the word in a droning fashion. "I…I need to be, not here. I need to be home. Need to be…" He shakes his head. "Long. Long way home."

Eddy takes a single step forward. "I have no idea what you're talking about, alright? But if you want to go home, I can take you there. We'll go back to the apartment, and everything will be fine."

"Where?"

"The apartment. We were just there." Eddy takes another few steps forward. "Do you have your goodly amulet on?"

Adrastos just blinks. His face is empty, his hands at his side. He almost looks like he's sleepwalking.

Eddy is near the parking lot island now. "Can I call you Blank?"

"What?"

"Just so I have something to call you."

"What? I need…"

"To go home?"

Blank finally focuses on Eddy, looking her in the eyes. "Yes…"

"Then I'll take you." Eddy steps up on the island and grabs him by the shoulders. "Don't move." She checks under the collar of his shirt, lifting it from side to side. There is no goodly amulet. "Dammit," she mutters.

"Here," Blank says, seemingly in reply, even though he doesn't move at all.

Eddy ignores him and adjusts the clasp on her own goodly amulet, letting the extra length of the chain unloop and expand the size of the necklace, making it big enough for two. She hesitates just a moment before putting the chain around Adrastos's neck. Eddy is pretty sure this entity has to be a new member of the system, but if not, if this is a symptom of something worse, she will be completely exposed to it once they are under joint protection.

But she has to. It's Adrastos. They're the closest thing to family she has now. Eddy slips the goodly charm over their head.

"There. But we gotta go. We need to get out of here. It's not safe this late at night."

Blank doesn't respond. His head droops, and one hand grips Eddy's arm above the elbow. His whole body shivers.

"Are you okay?" Eddy asks.

"*Here.*" The word is carried on a faint whisper, hardly a word at all.

Eddy bites her lip. "Okay. Okay, come on." She puts her arm around his shoulders.

She leads Blank along, heading toward the sidewalk as they begin the trip home. Blank himself is listless, easily guided as Eddy leads them both down the empty road. Eddy does not, will not, look over at the forest they had run through as they pass by it.

Soon, eventually, with shuffling feet and shivering arms, they reach the edge of the apartment complex. They slip between cars and up the walk, approaching their building. At the door, on the tiny porch, Blank squirms a few times as Eddy manages the goodly charm.

"What's wrong?" she asks, keeping her arm around him.

He doesn't answer. He breathes heavily a few times, but other than that, becomes still again.

Eddy is sprawled on her back on her bedroom floor. She had been reading *Infinite Break: The Invisible Emperor*, and she's almost finished. The paperback is right there beside her on the floor, so it only makes sense that she's reading it. She feels a little hungry, but it's getting late. Eating this close to sleep is bad for the metabolism, right? She reaches out for the book but stops in midair for a few moments, considering what to do. Maybe she will just make some tea instead. Her feet and legs are very cold. Tea and cards, good idea.

She grabs her tarot deck, and in the kitchen Eddy pours a mug of water and sets it in the microwave. Adrastos is in their room practicing a few cords on the guitar. That would be Noah. Eddy shuts the microwave door.

A few minutes pass. The water is still cold.

Eddy is just standing there, staring at the microwave. She blinks. What? She slowly glances to the side, looking at the wall by the kitchen table where the anomalous paper had been. The anomalous paper that is still hidden away in Adrastos's closet.

Shouldn't she, hang it…back up?

Tsunamis of pain are suddenly crashing over her brain, blotting out her vision for moments, minutes. She clutches her head and staggers to the side. She grasps the tarot deck from the table and stumbles toward the kitchen door. No, there's no door in this kitchen. The old kitchen had a door, the kitchen at her father's house. Eddy bumps into the couch and turns toward Adrastos's room.

"The, paper…" Eddy manages to choke out as she leans on their doorframe.

Adrastos is sitting in their desk chair, guitar on the ground, two fingers from each hand pressed against their closed eyeballs. Their face is screwed up, mouth in a grimace, legs twitching slightly.

"No, N-Noah." Eddy falls to her knees in front of them, spilling the deck across the floor, grabbing their wrists and pulling their hands away. "You have to stop. You can't keep hurting yourself like that."

They lean their head back a bit, eyes bloodshot, blinking rapidly. "I—I—I can't see."

"You're doing it to yourself, Noah."

"Daryl."

"Daryl? *Daryl*, dammit, what are you doing? Why are you doing this now? I thought you were okay now."

"I'm not. We're not." His voice is wavering, his hands shaking. "Everything is all blurred, and my head hurts so much, and everything is so bad. *Everything* is bad. I don't have a home anymore. I've been gone so long I can't even remember where my pack used to live."

"Dammit. Dammit, Daryl, this is why." Eddy presses her forehead against his chest, pulling his hands down farther from his face, trying to dispel the aching waves of pain in her own mind.

"No. It's something. Something else, this time. I just want to remember what it looked like!"

"You're gonna be fine. We just have to, have to get through this week. Let someone else front. I have my cards, I have my cards. But—but I have to get the paper. The paper Hawthorn gave us."

"Who?"

"DNA."

Daryl finally lowers his head, looking at Eddy, staring down at her hair. He tries to pull his hands free, but she won't release them.

"Let go," he says, teeth clenched.

"No. Daryl, no." She turns her face up to him. "I won't let you keep hurting yourself like before."

Daryl twists his hands, trying to slip his wrists from Eddy's fingers. "I won't. I don't do that. I protect us. I…wait." Daryl leans forward slightly, widening his eyes. "Why are you bleeding?"

"W-what?"

"Your lip. It's busted." Daryl frees one hand from Eddy's suddenly slack grip. He touches her bottom lip and blood is on his finger.

Eddy licks her lip, tasting rust. "No…" she says without any force behind the word. She releases Daryl's hand and crawls over to the closet, wrenching the door aside.

Every single page scattered across the floor is pure black. Darkness like oil that is spilling out and pooling around her hands and knees, pulling her forward into the depths and embracing her with tendrils across her arms, around her chest. No, no, no. She is drowning.

Expanse Three

Splinter 15

It takes a minute before Eddy can finally forcepull Blank into the apartment. He stumbles slightly over the threshold, his feet almost slipping on the still-damp mud from his shoes.

"Damn, we're both messes, aren't we?" Eddy asks more to herself than to Blank.

She has more mud on her body than Blank. Her feet and legs are covered in the viscous mass. As Eddy shuts the door, she takes the goodly amulet off from around Blank's neck. He stands there for a moment in the middle of the living room, simply looking at her.

"Come on, get your shoes off. We've got too much mud in here already." Eddy plops down on the floor, removing her shoes and socks and leaving them by the door. "Why did you even go to the library? Why there?"

Blank's eyes drift to the side, his head slowly following in a gentle tilt. He's breathing softly, chest rising and falling under his damp shirt.

Eddy stands up. "Do you know where you are?" She touches his shoulder.

"H-here."

Eddy forces a small laugh. "Well, yeah, I guess that is a correct answer. Um…"

Blank still has not taken off his shoes, has not even moved from the spot he seems rooted to. Eddy gently pushes on his chest, leading him to the couch and sitting him down. She crouches, untying his shoelaces.

Blank mutters something.

Eddy looks up. "What?"

"Here is not home." Blank swallows. "Here is not home. I'm tangled up in air. I can't hardly move. I need."

"I…I don't understand. Um, can you, I mean, what do you mean? Can you explain it better?"

"Mother," Blank whispers so softly Eddy almost doesn't catch it.

"You—you stop that." Eddy's heart starts bubbling in her chest, and her lungs quickly begin to expand, increasing in and out like a bilge pump.

"I need. I need, I need, I *need*." Blank fidgets violently, jerking one leg up, striking Eddy in the mouth with a foot still in its shoe.

"Ay!" Eddy tumbles backward, catching herself with one hand on the ground behind her. "Dammit…*dammit*." She presses the back of her hand against her lower lip. "What was that for!"

Blank's knees are curled against his chest, and he is shivering like a buoy in turbulent waters.

Eddy lifts her hand away for a moment and sees the blood across her skin. She stands and covers her lip again. "Okay. Just—just stay right there." She walks a few paces diagonally past the couch, moving toward her bedroom. "Hopefully someone else will front real soon. Give you the welcoming tour or something. Harold? Harold, can you hear me?" Eddy raises her voice as if it might help, despite the growing headache pooling inside her brain. "Is *anyone* over shoulder?"

Blank ceases his shuddering. He turns his head toward Eddy, looking right past her, eyes swollen and wide with some sort of surging emotion. His mouth drops open, and a faintest, "Nooo…" trickles from his lips.

Eddy keeps backing up toward her room. "What? What is—?" She bumps into something in the doorway.

Everything inside her stops. Her chest is being crushed; her head is cracking open like a glacier. The bedroom hallway in her father's house is superimposed on her vision, and she can't get her balance. She's stuck leaning in the divide of her doorway, too far in to be against the door, but too far out to see anything behind her at all.

Then nothing. Eddy is falling backward through empty space that was filled, was filled not even a moment ago. Carpets are never soft enough.

Eddy awakens with a moan. It's morning. Why is she sleeping on the couch? That, leak in her room, right? Over her bed. It's keeping her awake at night. Did they fix it yet? She did put in the work order. But…when did she do that exactly? Why does her mouth hurt?

She rolls over to the side, chilly from not even having blankets. That was a stupid idea, just sleeping in her clothes. Not warm enough. Eddy sits up, stretching her back and cracking it once. Oh, all the anomalous paper is here on the floor in front of her, too. Why did Hawthorn even bother with them? They are entirely empty. Maybe he had gotten them mixed up with regular paper. That would be funny. Does she have work today?

No.

"Eddy!"

She jumps slightly, turning her head toward Adrastos's room. "Gods, you scared me."

"Come here! Come here now!"

That sounds, bad. Eddy rises and pushes their door open slightly, peaking into their room. "What is it?"

Adrastos is sitting on their legs, wearing just underwear and a shirt, staring down at scattered typewritten pages all around them on the floor. "We…we, none of us did this!" They flail their arms around a moment.

"What are you talking about? Who is it?"

"Hanna. Everyone else is panicking. Something is happening. We don't know." She sobs, and it catches in her throat. Her lip quivers a moment before she continues. "Noah's the worst right now. He's gone back, way back, hiding somewhere. Daryl is trying to find him. He said no one go after Noah but him. I don't know where Harold is. Stanly's here, though. I can't, I *can't*." Hanna hops up and staggers backward into the wall, pressing flat against it.

"It—it's okay. Um, you're gonna be fine. It's just…" A hairline fissure begins cracking across Eddy's mind, as if something was there, just under the ice. Something sunken but still there. She presses her hands against her temples and looks down. Mud. There is mud on her jeans, mud on the floor, mud on her scattered tarot cards. "I…oh gods. Oh gods!" Eddy falls to her knees as a deluge of memories from last night smash through her mind, ripping her away from this moment. That's why. That's why her mouth hurts. And, and the papers! They were…! No, they weren't. They *can't* have been. They were fine just a minute ago, as pure white as when Hawthorn had brought them. But her cards!

"No…no, no." Eddy scoops up a single handful of cards, each one soft from the water—melting between her fingers—the images covered over in dirt, and they're ruined.

"This is really not okay, okay?" Adrastos says through clenched teeth. That's how Stanly talks. Eddy has only seen him front a handful of times.

"Stanly? Stanly, why is there so much mud? Where did Hanna go?" Eddy still has one hand against her head as she looks up at him with one eye open. There was never this much mud at her home before, at her father's house. She should go back.

"I couldn't tell you! And she ran off. Couldn't take it! By god, I can't either!" He grips one hand over his chest. "Heaven help us."

"Stop! Stop, tell me what's going on!" Eddy forces herself back to her feet, crinkling the handful of cards into a ball in her fist.

"I cannot, okay? I'm just not able to. No, I haven't even been here that long. I know the absolute least about this system hullabaloo! There's nothing I can do, okay? Okay?"

"Stop! You know what Adrastos stands for!"

Their body slumps forward slightly, but before it falls, the body becomes rigid again. "He said it himself," they whisper. "Been here the least amount of time. Its meaning hasn't sunk in yet."

What? Noah, Daryl, Harold, Hanna, Stanly, that's…that's everyone. Everyone in—oh. Oh, Eddy remembers.

"L-Lili? *Lili*?" She has never seen Lili front before, not in the five years she's known the Adrastos System.

"We do have a…slight problem, it seems." Lili stands with her head slightly inclined, stretching and flexing her fingers in front of her. "Seems a bit focused on Noah.

That's why Daryl is so concerned. So concerned about his little Noah."

"…what?"

Lili just chuckles a moment. "Never mind, child. You have Philip to be concerned with now." She smirks mildly and then notices the tarot cards clenched in Eddy's hand. "Oh, child, what happened to your grandmother's cards?"

"I don't know. I can hardly remember. But they're ruined. Gone." Eddy glances down at them. "We brought in too much mud or…something…"

Lily just shakes her head and begins walking slowly toward the door. "A pity. But as for us, there is someone or something new within our group. I am leaning toward the latter." She leaves out the room.

Eddy doesn't follow at first. She wants to punch something. To tear up all the soggy earth in the world and throw it into a fire. She throws the wad of cards back onto the floor. "*Dammit!*"

"I suspect you have more pressing issues to worry about than those cards now," Lili calls out from elsewhere in the apartment.

Eddy rubs her mouth and it still hurts. She sighs and leaves the room, looking for Lili. "Maybe, I mean, I just remembered a few minutes ago, remembered part of what happened last night." The bathroom light is on, and Lili is standing inside before the mirror, shirt dropped onto the floor. "There's some new person. He said he doesn't have a name. I just called him Blank. He seemed really confused. Hasn't anyone talked to him?"

"No, no one claims to have done so at all. We cannot find it. Not inside the headspace anywhere. Certainly, it must *be*; however, it does not manifest itself as a *being*. This leads me to think it is something else. This *Blank*, as you have named it, seems…'inserted,' if that is the word I am trying to say." Lili leans toward the mirror. "My, my…how quickly this body ages." She raises her head, lightly trailing her fingers over the body's throat as she studies it in the glass.

Eddy stands outside the bathroom doorway, partially obscured by the frame. "I don't understand. It…" Eddy swallows. "It's bad if you're fronting, isn't it?"

"How do you mean?" Lili turns around with a small smile on her lips, her hands resting on the counter behind her, leaning back slightly. "Bad me, or bad situation?"

"Situation," Eddy says quickly. "Bad situation, I mean." She doesn't like this Lili.

"Child. I only tell you this next part because I have grown rather fond of this little…asylum here." She holds out her left hand a minute, considering the chewed off fingernails. Her mouth puckers and frowns, almost like a pout. "From my experience and my knowledge of these things, I can only say your Blank is a tulpa. An odd one at that. Accidental, I might even say. Born of a command unable to take root. Perhaps this is the effect of mind control over a nonsingular mind." Lili looks up at Eddy with only her eyes and whispers, "Unprecedented."

"So, you're saying, someone…something, tried to mind control Adrastos?"

"A guess. But I am a good guesser."

"Have you told them? Any of them? Harold, he—he'll know what to do, right?"

"I will not tell them. You will. I am only here because they are willing to accept anyone. People other systems would usually block out. They are perhaps kind, but it is also a necessity that they are not choosy. I shall extend equal courtesy, but no more." Lili pushes off the counter and brushes past Eddy at the doorway. "Don't forget that word."

"Tulpa?"

"Good girl." Lili continues toward Adrastos's room. "I shall retire now, as the others have, though that is putting it nicely. The body will sleep." She closes the door.

For a while, Eddy doesn't move. She is breathing softly and doesn't shake. She will go and hang the anomalous papers back up, and perhaps—just maybe—she should tell Hawthorn what Lili has said.

What more could drive you? What less could stop you? Striding, striving Which place could you more rightly call a home? I am not born into this, blindly.

Binding. Trapped between your yous. Mantled and mounted, bridled drawn. Dawn will not come for us. This place is [redacted] without air, with out lungs. Without of place; I am not here.

Here.

Running is not the way out between these growing columns, pillars, bars. Closing in on your feet and curshing between your marrow. Please. /Please/ don't follow us here. Usher out your memories and never again travers these grounds.

These teeth will knash// ypu to pieces. You. You will never find me here.

Splinter 16

Eddy is in the men's bathroom at work, locked in a stall and crying.

She's softly knocking her forehead against the wall as she keeps trying to ignore the fact that this is the men's room. That this is her only means of retreat.

The restaurant is so busy this lunch shift. Too busy. Eddy's inundated with six tables waiting on her return, but nothing she does is enough. She can't be fast enough, she can't be informative enough, she can barely keep herself from screaming because of it all. A mother had come in with her small child, a daughter, not more than five years old. Eddy had done her best, done everything she could.

She gave them the best service out of all her tables. She brought extra crayons for the daughter. Eddy had not even charged for the milk refill. But what did she get in return?

Nothing.

Not a single cent, and it's all so pointless. Nothing she does is enough. It feels like struggling through molasses.

She doesn't care what happens now; she doesn't care.

The door opens. "Eddy? Are you in here?"

It's one of her coworkers. She thinks for a moment that maybe if she just stays silent enough, he will pass her by and no one will ever bother her again. She could lurk in the rafters and storage closets by day and at night creep into the kitchen to steal food and drinks, and this restaurant on the corner of North Pearl and West Magnolia Streets would forever wonder why food went missing when they count inventory at the end of each week.

"Yes." Eddy's voice cracks.

"Karyn's looking for you. Why didn't you tell anyone you're in here? All your tables need you and are getting mad." He's standing outside the stall now. "Are you taking a shit?"

"No. No." Eddy sniffs and wipes an eye. "I'll be out. Just—just a minute."

"Karyn needs you *now*." He leaves the bathroom.

Karyn, second in command. Eddy knows she's going to get fired for this, knows that Karyn will not accept any excuses for this—as if Eddy has anything besides excuses to explain this. Sure, she could throw up a fog of tales and words about DNA and memories and drowning in all these expectations, demands. But it will be no use. It will be no use and she will no longer inhabit this place, this building. Eddy *knows* it.

With one last shuddering breath, Eddy leaves the bathroom.

Karyn is waiting just outside, hands in fists on her hips. "Eddy! I have Fabiano taking care of your tables. The bar's slow. What are you doing? Why didn't you tell anyone you were going off the floor? Do you know how many discounts it took to settle down your guests?"

Eddy just shakes her head and rubs an eye again. "I'm sorry. I just…I just, I couldn't."

Karyn raises her eyebrows a bit and drops her arms to her sides. "Are you crying? What's wrong?"

"Just…stuff. Lots of stuff. Happening, I mean."

Karyn sighs. "Why didn't you tell me this? Tell me you needed a minute and get your tables covered. Or tell me when you came in. I could've worked with you."

"I—I dunno." Eddy sniffs. "I just needed—"

"Hold up, look, normally you're a good server, but you've been slipping up hard recently, and this isn't acceptable. What am I supposed to do right now?"

"I dunno." Eddy says softly.

"Darn it, Eddy, I have to write you up for this at the least. Give all your open tables to Fabiano and go home. I'll call you tomorrow to let you know if we'll need you the rest of the week."

"But—but I *need* the money."

"Don't we all." Karyn shakes her head. "I can't let that come at the expense of our guests. In a perfect world, we wouldn't even be having this conversation. I'll call you. Now go home."

Eddy is soaked from the rain during her walk back. It wasn't raining when she went to work, so she didn't bring her broken umbrella. She unlocks the apartment door and slips inside, water dripping off her onto the carpet.

Inside is dark; Adrastos is still asleep. Eddy takes her shoes off as quietly as she can and decides a shower might do her good: a short time when she can just let herself forget about everything.

Once when Eddy was much younger, she got a double ear infection and could hardly hear anything. But showering during that week was the weirdest part. It was nicer in a way. It created more focus on the feel of the water, the way it massaged her skin and streamed down her body. And when she leaned her head backward to rinse out her hair it sounded like a slop of worms over her skull. Perhaps that wasn't the best way to describe it—because she liked the sound—but it was and still is the only way she can think to explain the experience.

Since then Eddy has always worn earplugs when she showers and simply cleans her ears afterward with a small washcloth.

Today Eddy lets the water run hotter than normal, forcing herself to focus on it alone. But also the air feels more cold today; the draft is coming in aggressively through the ajar door and between the openings in the curtain. She shivers and turns the water hotter still. With her eyes closed, she lets it pelt her chest and run down her body, over her penis, along the skin that is not her own.

Some muffled sound comes past her earplugs, desiring to be heard. Eddy opens her eyes and sees the shadow of someone across the curtain. She jumps and gasps, almost slipping on the wet surface. She tears out an earplug.

"Eddy," the voice is raised but not yelling, "you're home early."

Adrastos.

Eddy peeks around the curtain and sees them standing there in underwear only. "Daryl?"

"Yeah."

"Dammit, you scared me."

"Sorry."

"What is it?"

"Why are you home early?"

Eddy doesn't immediately reply. "Just…bad day." She lets the curtain fall back into place and turns back to the water.

"Are you gonna be much longer?" Daryl asks.

"Why?"

"We need to shower too. Don't use all the hot water."

"Oh. Right. Sorry." The apartment only has one bathroom, and she's not actually showering to clean herself right now. She turns the water off. "Close your eyes."

Daryl is silent.

"Are your eyes closed?"

"Yeah, they are."

"Good."

Eddy pulls back the curtain and grabs her towel. She wraps it around herself and walks past Daryl out of the bathroom. "I dunno how much hot water is left."

"I'll be quick." The water turns on again.

"Wait." Eddy stands at the door, not looking in. "Tell Harold I need to talk to him after you're done."

"Sure."

Eddy finishes drying off in her room and puts on a bathrobe, tying the fabric belt in front of her. Hawthorn is coming back tomorrow to finish his diagnosis. Both she and Adrastos have been turning on the EVP recorder at night, but beyond that nothing seems to have changed at all. The rehung anomalous papers are still as white and unmarked as the first day. Was there even anything here to discover? There is Blank.

She can't tell Hawthorn about him, though. Hawthorn already indicated he would overlook the Adrastos System in his diagnosis, and besides, it's none of his business if Adrastos happened to gain a new member or not.

But Lili had said Blank was a tulpa, not a member proper. How important is that? Eddy doesn't even know what exactly a tulpa is. She should go to the library and look it up. She definitely has time to now. Eddy groans and goes to the kitchen.

She prepares a cup of tea and is sipping the hot liquid when the shower stops. All is silent for a moment, the curtain is pulled open, wet feet, some brushing of fabric. Daryl walks out into the main area with the towel in hand instead of on him.

"Oh," Eddy says quietly into her mug.

This is certainly not the first time she's seen Daryl naked, but it is the first time she has seen him naked in this apartment. She lets her eyes linger on him.

"What will the others say?" Eddy asks with a slight smile.

"They don't have a say right now. I'm a werewolf. I ain't got no modesty." He lifts the towel to finish drying his hair.

"Don't I know." Her tea is still too hot, so she sets it behind her on the counter she is leaning on.

"Besides, I know you don't mind either. Eduardo." He drops the towel on the floor and enters the kitchen, standing in front of her.

Eddy shakes her head. "Don't use that."

"Yeah, sorry. But you know, it's not hard to be naked," Daryl says softly. "You just, take everything off." He reaches down with both hands and starts untying Eddy's bathrobe.

"Hey." She puts her hands over his, holding them, stopping them.

"Fair's fair." He waits.

Eddy glances down, both at his groin and at his hands in hers. She licks her lips and can practically hear her mother's voice floating through her head saying, *El que calla, otorga.* Several seconds pass. Eddy drops her hands to her sides. "Only for you."

Daryl smiles and finishes untying the cord. For a moment Eddy's robe hangs on her shoulders, only a sliver of skin showing between the two halves. Daryl pushes the fabric aside at the collar and reveals her naked body. Eddy leans forward, allowing Daryl to push the robe all the way back. It falls to the floor behind her.

They stand together a minute, not talking. Just looking.

"You still look good," Daryl finally says.

"It's not right. I should at least have breasts."

"Obviously I like you better without." He steps back and crosses his arms. "You should show off more. Even if it is a guy's body, it's still really good. I think so. You should be proud."

Eddy shrugs and looks away. "No, I just…can't."

Daryl tilts his head slightly to the side.

"You are the only one fronting, right?" Eddy asks.

He nods. "I promise."

"Well." Eddy crouches down, picking up the bathrobe again and putting one arm into it. "Satisfied?"

"Mostly."

Eddy rolls her eyes and puts her other arm into the robe, tying it tight. "Isn't that what Mel's for now?"

"He's just a thing. Not serious."

She turns, standing sideways to Daryl, and picks up her tea. "I still need to talk to Harold. Lili told me something about Blank." She glances at him. "Did you get Noah back?"

Daryl furrows his brows slightly, his lips tight. "Yeah. I got him. He said he was going to try to take a nap. I guess I'll go check on him when Harold takes over fronting."

Eddy is silent a moment, then turns to face him completely. "Are you and him a thing?"

"*What*?" Daryl takes a step back. "No. I'm just…you know, looking after him."

"Like that doesn't sound fucking suspicious as fuck." She jabs a finger into his chest. "Noah's too innocent for you. You better at least get rid of Mel."

"It's not like that." Daryl raises his hands slightly. "He's just the most affected by this Blank person. The whole group wants me to look after him."

Eddy snorts. "Yeah, right. Let me just talk to Harold."

"Sure. Fine." Adrastos blinks a few times and lowers his arms. "Eddy."

"Harold?"

"Speaking."

Eddy shakes her head and turns her back to him. "Your towel's on the floor. Daryl was being Daryl again."

"Wha—? Oh! Gods." He grabs up the towel and wraps it proper. "You can turn around now."

"Why were you all freaking out so much over Blank?"

"Blank…" he says the word slowly, as if examining it with his tongue. "Yes, much to our shame, he rather left us scattering." He pauses. "I think we're okay now. The main problem was we didn't know who or where Blank was, though I guess we still don't for that matter. But at least he won't take us by surprise again."

"But how could someone else front without you guys knowing it?"

"It's not like there's some control room, Eddy. No captain's chair with a steering wheel and dashboard. When we front it's wherever we are inside the house that is effectively this body's mind. Fronting is just this, sort of, bubble around us. And it takes a little concentration to handle the perceptions of the body outside overlaid onto our individual body perceptions inside at the same time. If someone's nearby, they can look over shoulder, but if we're not fronting, we don't instantly know who does have that 'bubble' around them."

"Hmm." Eddy scratches her chin. "You know, Lili said Blank is probably a tulpa."

"A what?"

"My thoughts exactly," Eddy mumbles. "Why don't you go ask her?"

"You know I can't do that. She spends all her time way back in the headspace. She talks to us, oh, maybe once a year."

"So, that's it? You can't just go talk to her yourself?"

"No. Out of my power at least. Maybe Stanly. He's been here about two years, but despite that she usually talks to him now when she talks to us. I doubt he could turn up much, though." Harold shrugs.

"Okay, fine. Whatever. So do we tell Hawthorn?"

"Tell Hawthorn what?"

"About Blank."

"Why would we? As far as I can tell, he's purely incidental to the botched voiding."

Eddy doesn't bring up the point again that none of them are sure who Blank is.

"Besides," Harold continues, "we rather like the privacy of anonymity." He walks into their bedroom.

Eddy follows. The carpet is still clearly stained from the mud, even though they cleaned up what they could and thrown it all to the trash, the same as Eddy's cards. Removed from this place.

"Hawthorn's coming back tomorrow. If we do need a voiding, do you think he'll find out?" Eddy asks.

"With these papers and recordings, I would certainly hope so." Harold glances back at Eddy. "Do stand out at the door please."

"Oh, yeah. Sorry." Eddy steps outside the bedroom and stands with her back to the open door. "What about Daryl?"

"What about him?" Clothing is being shuffled around.

"He's looking after Noah?"

"Yes. He volunteered even, and we all agreed. Noah seemed the most shaken up by Blank's appearance."

"Why?"

"I don't know. His irrational fear of strangers perhaps. You know how he doesn't like talking to people. Maybe he's just afraid of getting less attention in the system."

"No, I mean, why is Daryl looking after Noah?"

"Why not? He cares about Noah's well-being. Completely fancies himself as the protector of the group, but you know that, don't you?"

"Yeah." Eddy sighs. "I just, I dunno. What do you think about intersystem relationships?"

"Both of the women here are rather…not my type."

Eddy turns around. Harold is dressed and pulling on a sweater. "Not you. Wouldn't it get weird?"

"You're not in the system. You won't have to worry about it." He sits down at the desk and sighs as he lifts the typewriter over onto the shelves nearby. He opens up the notebook he uses to keep track of their spending, then picks up some crumpled fast-food receipts from the desk and frowns. "I told Daryl to stop eating out."

He flicks the small receipts behind him and spins around in the desk chair. "I would like to add something, since we're on the topic. Hanna here for the moment." She smiles and looks at Eddy. "Daryl is just animal enough that I would certainly sleep with him. Preferably in his wolf form." She snickers.

"Um…okay. I know Daryl wouldn't be interested, though. On, well, two accounts."

"Ah! I may be old enough to be your grandmother, but age is hardly something to be scoffed at. Besides, if Daryl's claims are true, then he's forty-eight years old himself, aside from looking much younger on account of the lycanthropy and all." She keeps spinning the chair round and round.

"And Noah's fifteen," Eddy mutters.

"Isn't he, indeed?" Hanna grins. "Too bad. Even one out of two components isn't enough, is it Harold? But that's how it always goes. The more specific the kink, the harder it is to manage." She snickers, then stamps their feet onto the floor, stopping the chair from spinning. "I really wish she wouldn't do that. She needs to stop blabbering."

"You're back, Harold?"

"Yes." He glances at the desk and groans when he sees the receipts are gone.

"On the floor," Eddy says quietly as she points. "Also, I think those are Noah's from the smoothies he's been getting."

Harold hops off the chair and collects up the receipts. "How is he buying them without talking to the cashier?"

"Daryl buys them for him."

"Hmph! They are trying to bankrupt us, I swear. All of them." He rubs a hand over his mouth and falls back into the desk chair. "Would you please slap them next time you see either of those two buy something?"

"Yeah, sure, because that's a good idea. Isn't positive reinforcement supposed to be better?"

"Either way, you can 'positively' reinforce Daryl or Noah all you want, but we're a little off topic now. There are only two things for us to do about this Blank: take a look into what a tulpa is, and be ready to greet our newest member when he finally decides to announce himself."

iffff you touch me
don;t listen tome, dont,
i am covered in sharp edges
my
my, i, sharper than

like the cut on a broard thrown
sideways, over hills and fens,i
sharper than, sharper,,
dont
tree branches twitch when skys
fading wind wont/dont/pick up higher
higee,,,,only the tips,tops,will
move in my windy planes,flat empty
plains,, and i cnat see you, here,
can;t
i am stammering your, fingers breaki ng
dont, i,
don,t

Splinter 17

Hawthorn is sitting at the kitchen table, playing one of the EVP tapes with headphones over his ears. He had arrived early before lunch to wrap things up. Eddy is sitting on the couch armrest, twisting a bit of her shirt between her fingers. Noah is in their room, staying exceptionally silent.

Hawthorn hits the stop button on that cassette player. He just sits there for a moment, staring down at the two other cassettes resting on the table. With a slight sigh he lifts the headphones and lays them across the table.

"These three are the only tapes?" he asks.

Eddy nods. "What's on them?"

Hawthorn leans back and folds his arms, a slow movement, one he doesn't seem to want to finish. But he does, and he looks up, and he says, "Nothing."

"N-nothing?"

"No. Not a single thing."

They're both silent. Noah strums a single cord on his guitar, and Eddy glances in his direction.

Hawthorn pushes himself up. "There's nothing for me to put in my report. All DNA protocol says nothing is here. There's nothing to void out, nothing to contain or take care of. The emergency responders were correct the first time."

"But…but how? I mean—" Eddy swallows, suddenly feeling like she might cry. *Please don't fucking cry.* "Why doesn't it *feel* like nothing is here?"

"I'm really sorry." Hawthorn puts a hand on her shoulder for a moment. Then he turns back to the table and begins packing the equipment up. "Nothing here has been abnormal. Not a single reading, no temperatures, no EVPs. Even the anomalous papers are so untouched I could reuse them. There's literally nothing I can do."

"You have to do something," she whispers.

"I can't." He doesn't look at her.

A moment of thought, and she says, "I'll tell them. I'll tell them you broke protocol. That you took that crystal out. That you still think you're a druid."

Hawthorn freezes, the last wall thermometer in his hand hovering over the bag. He sets it on the table and turns around. "That won't help you."

"I don't care." Her voice breaks. "We need *something*."

Hawthorn puts his fingers over his eyes and leans back slightly, inhaling deeply. He drops his arms. "Look. DNA, it…it isn't great. I know. Believe me, I know. Their approach is totally different. There's nothing I can do. Nothing. If I break protocol, they'll revoke my license, and I don't have any other skill sets. There's nothing else in the whole world I can do besides menial labor. I tried to help. I really did. I wouldn't have gone that extra step to help if I had known you'd throw it back in my face."

Eddy winces and looks down at the floor. "I…" She doesn't know what to say.

A moment or two pass.

"She didn't mean it," Noah says in a small voice, standing at the doorframe with his face half-hidden.

Hawthorn raises an eyebrow as he crosses his arms. "Oh. But I know." He nods, a small gesture, barely bobbing his face up and down. "I've been doing this long enough to know. Officially, there's nothing else I can do. But I can still do something unofficially. Only if you promise that you won't tell anyone. Got it?"

Eddy nods quickly. "I'm sorry. Yes. Please."

The druid takes out a piece of paper and a pen. "This is my pager number. My personal pager. Give me a call if anything else happens or you get something concrete. If it's really serious—like life threatening—I could do something unofficially. Get it worked out later. Otherwise, concrete evidence, and I can get a new, official case opened. That's what I can do." He holds out the small scrap of paper.

Eddy reaches up with one shaking hand and takes it. She holds it tight, instinctively balling her fist, crumpling it between her fixed fingers. "Thank you."

"This is why I became a druid years ago. To give back. Not for DNA." He packs away the last thermometer and hefts the bag over a shoulder. "And it's a pager. Call me anytime."

"Wait," Noah says. "What…what about a tulpa?"

Hawthorn lowers the bag. "A tulpa? What do you mean, 'what about a tulpa?' "

"What is it?"

"Hm, well." Hawthorn begins speaking a bit slower. "Not something I've encountered firsthand. They're associated with Eastern practices of enlightenment and holy men. The idea has also migrated to Western traditions, but it's generally known as a thoughtform in that context. Basically they're a constructed nonphysical entity usually created by focused mental energy. Why do you ask?"

Noah just shrugs his shoulders.

"Is it…important?" Hawthorn ventures, looking at Noah and then Eddy.

Eddy averts her face from him, instead glancing at Noah and letting him lead.

Noah shakes his head. "We don't know. We don't think so. Just thought you would know what it is."

"Listen here, if you're holding anything back, I need to know. I already know you're a multiple, and that's not a big deal. But if you know anything, anything at all, you have to tell me so I can help."

"It's not me." Noah takes a step back.

"I didn't say that."

"There isn't anything here. Eddy will tell you if there is." He shuts the bedroom door.

Hawthorn takes a half step toward them, but stops himself. "Eddy, even the smallest detail could help." He isn't looking at her.

"I don't know," she says softly.

The DNA agent turns away and opens the front door. "I guess there's nothing else I can do, then. Just, page me, if anything comes up."

"Okay."

He steps out. It's raining: heavy torrents sweeping sideways in sheets and droves, assailing the world like a million battle-frenzied warriors. Hawthorn walks out, unfazed, and shuts the door.

Noah is lying on the bed when Eddy opens the door slightly, peeking into their room. His arms are splayed out above his head—holding Daryl's folding knife—and he's staring at the ceiling.

"Can I come in?"

"Yeah." He continues staring up.

Eddy steps over the typewriter on the floor, takes the heavy guitar case off their chair, and sets it aside before sitting down. "Why did you ask Hawthorn about tulpas if you didn't want to tell him about Blank?"

"I dunno. I was curious. I didn't want to wait for the library to open to go try to find it. It would've been hard to find, I bet. If even Harold didn't know it, how would I find it?"

"Harold doesn't know absolutely everything."

"It seems like it. He acts like it." He flicks the knife open.

"Well, yeah. He is really good." Eddy gently reaches out and takes the knife from Noah's fingers. "He knows how to keep things organized. He's a good core, a good leader for you all. Even though Daryl hogs the spotlight by fronting so much." She looks down at the blade before slowly clicking it shut.

"He's with me now."

"W-what? Who?"

"Daryl." Noah grips a small bit of the bedsheet between his fingers and rubs the crinkled fabric together.

"Oh."

They are both silent for nearly a minute, just staying together in the silence that only nighttime provides.

Noah coughs a moment, then says, "They keep telling me this isn't a problem, but…"

"What isn't?"

Noah just raises a hand slowly, pointing at the ceiling. "That. We really should get it fixed, don't you think?"

Eddy follows his gesture, eyes trailing up his hand and finger to the patch of black mold festering on the ceiling. Eddy gasps. The spores have grown around a constant leak, drips of water falling each second from on high and soaking Noah and his bed. That's right. Noah is drenched right now. The plaster ceiling is bubbling out, threatening to collapse in a small single-foot circle, to belch out its accumulated fluid and gestating fungus in a race against time forced by evolutionary competition. Get there. Get everywhere. *Grow* everywhere.

"Oh! Shit, damn, that's really"—she looks back down at Noah and blinks—"really…I dunno."

Noah turns his head to her and smiles. "Yeah, me either." He chuckles. "This place is nice. It's a good apartment."

"For our price range, at least."

"Yeah." Noah looks back up at the ceiling and moans softly.

"Are you okay?" Eddy asks. "You sound like you might be getting sick."

"I…no, I think I'm okay. But, you know what I think?"

"What?"

"I think, I think there are very dark corners in certain places. And I'm afraid we're in one of the darkest there can be."

"…what?"

"I dunno." He gives a small shrug. "I dunno."

Eddy purses her lips and stands, ruffling his hair. "Try to get some sleep."

"That's hard."

"I know. I'll see you tomorrow." Eddy drops the knife on the desk.

As she walks back to her room, her bare feet squelch with each step on the waterlogged carpet.

Like a tsumami; you crush me. You
many, you few.. Scaping through you
and me; I sm not here;

Nothign you or I or we.
Can do. Perculate through mt skin
and wash me out, away, gone from
here. Pecular presperation, pardon my
presets and promis no participati-
on.

Persipitation will settle
in my soul and fill me with nothing,
bloating with pain. Your pain. I
feel you. I can feel nothing but you.
You. Hollow me out a million
million
times and I will still be you. Still
be between you. Please. /Please.?/
If I have no plave , no home ,
no promis, no.
I am not to be here. I. We. ##He##
IT is not the hign to fidn. IT is
not the thing hidddn. Hiding i s not
your answe r even if it s ould be./..
Should;nt be.
Might be.
Salvation will drip through your
fingers everytime you happen-grasp it.

Splinter 18

Eddy's restaurant, about ten blocks from the apartment complex, still hasn't called her. Perhaps they won't call her. Earlier in the day Eddy had longed for her tarot cards, longed for something to give some modicum of guidance. But right now she isn't thinking about that. Philip is over at the apartment again. He had commented on how clean the apartment looks today, and Eddy admits she vacuumed and tidied up a bit.

They are eating pizza in her room. Philip is going to spend the night.

They ate pizza. Now they're curled together on Eddy's bed. Talking.

"I've been trying to save up for a car," Eddy is saying. "It's so hard, though. There's always something we have to spend extra money on."

"Tell me about it. I'm struggling just to pay off my current car. I'm glad the rain has slowed down over this last week. When it rains I always get so nervous about driving. If I wreck it and it can't be fixed, then all this money will have gone to nothing."

"What about insurance?"

"I just have the minimum. It covers the other person, not me."

"That's stupid."

"I know." Philip squeezes her a bit tighter. "I'll get better insurance eventually. Right now I just have to be careful. Avoid any wrecks before they happen." He forces a small chuckle.

"I've always been afraid of that," Eddy says softly.

"What?"

"People dying."

"Well…yeah. I would think so."

"It's something I think about sometimes."

"The same way you think about people being crushed sometimes?"

Eddy is silent a moment. "Kinda. But worse than that. I mean, it's like…like, death has never touched me yet." She hesitates again and continues, slowly at first, but it all comes tumbling out after it gets going, like a dam crack breaking into a torrential wall of water. "I'm almost twenty-five years old, and death hasn't touch me at all. No one's died. Not even a coworker. I…I get really worried sometimes. Worried that death is just saving up for me. Saving up until it unleashes something really horrible on my life. On the people around me." Her voice drops. "It really scares me."

Philip doesn't respond.

"I'm sorry, I'm sorry. I shouldn't be talking about this."

"It—it's okay." Philip strokes her hair. "There's a lot of shit in the world, I know. It's okay, if—if you need to get it off your chest."

"Thanks." Eddy doesn't say anything after that.

Several minutes pass. Philip ventures, "My father disappeared."

"When?"

"When I was twelve. The very next year I wasn't allowed to see my uncle anymore, so that was hard. Like losing two people. I know it's not the same thing, but it's the same effect, not even being able to see them."

Eddy sniffs. "My mom and sister are gone."

"What? But I thought you said…?"

"They didn't, die. They left. Well, my mom left. My parents got a divorce almost a decade ago. She took my sister and left. Left me with my father. Left us both behind. She was the one who wanted the divorce. But why? I've never understood it."

"Why she left?"

"Why she left me."

"Oh." Philip hugs her a bit tighter again. "I'm sorry."

Eddy feels like she's floating, rocking gently as Philip rubs his hand up and down her thigh. The sun has set by now.

"Do you believe them?" Philip asks.

"Who?"

"The Adrastos System? Do you believe they really are multiple people in one brain? All controlling the same body?"

"They don't control the body all at the same time. They take turns fronting."

"You know what I mean."

The rain is falling so gently outside Eddy's window. She should open it and let the sticky air fill up the house and be like glue to all the books, the salt, their skin stuck to clothes. Philip is humming softly, quite content.

"I do believe them. I really do. It doesn't matter how they work. If they say that's what they are, then I believe them. I love them."

"Why do you love them? Don't you love me?"

Eddy is humming now too, in sync with Philip.

"They're beautiful," she says. "They're so like me, and I've known them for so long that no other part can really matter. I can't imagine my life without them. And of course I love you, too, but not as much as them, just because it hasn't been as long. But it's not the same. I love Adrastos differently than I love you."

"And I love you differently than I loved my uncle. Differently than I love the forest."

"The forest?"

"The woods. The wild untamed places where light barely filters down through the branches and leaves, with twigs and grass crunching beneath your feet."

Eddy laughs. "You sound like Daryl." She rolls over, over on Philip and over again with him on her. They keep rolling several times, eventually ending with Philip atop her.

"But I'm not Daryl. I'm Philip."

"I know. I know."

"Don't fall asleep," he says softly.

"I'm not."

"Are you sure?"

"Yes." Eddy smiles and nudges Philip in the chest with her elbow.

Everything is quiet in the apartment. Adrastos might be at Mel's house, but Eddy isn't sure. She doesn't think about Adrastos right now.

Philip kisses her, and they start making out again. A part of Eddy wants them to take it slow, but that gets overridden quickly. Very quickly. Philip is lying on top of Eddy and she presses her tongue into his mouth, sliding it over his teeth. The tips are round and smooth and she wonders if he had braces before. Braces like Daryl did. Correction, like the Adrastos System's body did. Philip slowly reaches down, pressing his hand against Eddy's hardened groin.

She turns her head from his lip and whispers, "Don't."

"Sorry. What is it? Too fast?" He pulls his hand away.

"No…I—I mean, it's not that." Eddy licks her lips.

"What is it?"

"I…I don't mind, it…really. It's just, I need you to know. I…" *Oh man. This is it. He's going to get up and leave.* "I'm not, really, actually…a guy."

"Uh…what? It sure feels like you are." Philip forces a two syllable chuckle.

"I mean. It's weird. I just, me, who I am, in my head, my body's not…I don't—I don't have a—a penis. I have a, you know, I have a, the other one." There is such a horrible twisting constriction in her stomach. A raw crushing like a tree root she had once seen growing through a small drain pipe: the whole thing had grown scrunched in, slowly cracking the edges of the pipe, but not fast enough to stop the strangulation.

Philip tilts his head to the side a bit. "A vagina?"

"Yeah."

"Like…trans?"

"Oh. You—you've heard of that?"

Philip nods. "Yeah. A little bit. Inside you feel like a girl?"

A woman.

"Yeah. But I'm pre-everything, so it doesn't show."

"Well, well, that's cool. That's fine. I actually don't mind."

"What? R-really?"

"Yeah. Totally fine by me. I identify more as pansexual anyway."

"What do you mean? Pansexual?"

"I mean I don't care about your body." He leans forward, pressing his forehead against hers. "I care about you."

"Oh. Wow."

Philip just chuckles. "I'm gonna guess this has been a problem before?" he whispers.

"…yeah."

"Well not with me."

Eddy breaks up into a grin. "I—I can't believe it."

"What?" He smiles too.

"That I met you."

"Well, I'm really glad we did, too." He brushes his nose against hers. "When did you realize you're trans?"

"In high school. My last year. Adrastos—Glen, actually helped a lot with that. And they made me feel less alone."

"I realized I'm pan back in high school too." Philip starts nibbling on Eddy's ear.

She shivers. The beginning of a headache is dribbling across her brain, pooling down in the base of her skull. She must be too tense, too excited. "Don't stop," she manages to squeak out between breaths.

Philip kisses her again, squeezing her sides, slowly moving his hands down. "I won't." His lips are still so close, brushing against hers. He reaches her waist, fingers digging under her waistband. "Can I record this?" His voice more air than sound.

What? That's weird. "Sure. Yes." *Just don't stop.*

Philip gets up from the bed for only a moment, clicking the camcorder on and leaving it on the desk pointing at them. He straddles Eddy again and they kiss and they kiss and he is slowly pulling down her pants.

Eddy gasps as Philip goes down, down, taking her inside him, using his lips and tongue. The spit rolling down his chin and the saliva on her groin cold against the air. Eddy moans too loudly, and she is so, so glad Adrastos isn't here. Can't hear. Can't see.

She raises her hips, roiling beneath him, turning slightly from side to side. It's been so long. Last time was in her room in her father's house, on the same sheets she'd had ever since she was little. It had been strange, like a point of no return.

This time it's still the wrong parts below her waist, but it doesn't matter. Not now. Right now it's working, the waves inside her surging up and back down, surging as she tangles her fingers in Philip's hair. Eddy arches her back one last time in surprise and pleasure, and she forgets everything else in the whole wide world for just a moment.

Philip coughs slightly and clears his throat before flopping down on top of her. "How was it?"

"G-good." Her breath hasn't quite caught up. "Really good." But she feels cold now. She doesn't mention this. She guesses it's the adrenaline.

Philip just nods and nuzzles his nose and face against her chest.

Eddy puts an arm over her eyes. "I can't believe we just did that."

"What?"

"Had sex on camera."

Philip laughs. "You did say okay." He pokes her gently.

"I know. I don't think I was paying attention." She turns her head to see the camcorder with its red light glowing on her desk. "Gods. This is so…oh gods."

"I'm sorry." Philip stands and turns the camcorder off. "Here. You can have the tape." He pops it out and leaves it on the desk. "There's nothing really important on here. Is that better?"

"Don't you mind?"

Philip shakes his head as he climbs back on top of Eddy, her pants still around her knees. "You're the one who's more exposed in it." He smiles. "Besides, I trust you."

these expectations will
push you flat
push you

unbalanced, i, and here
not even quarts can aline me,
i.
cdont follow, never fulfill
would yuo?
before you too
pushed flat

you
scatter/drift, over
me and me
eye

Splinter 19

The next day, after Philip has said a drawn-out farewell and Adrastos has already left to their job selling mattresses, Eddy is left alone in the apartment. The extra space in her bed feels all the more empty, the dirty pizza plates and glasses in the sink feel all the more abandoned. Eddy sits on the couch in the main room and holds her knees against her chest, waiting.

Maybe work will call her today. Maybe Hawthorn will call. Maybe Philip. She should make some tea and do her daily card reading and…but Eddy remembers she can't.

She shudders. She had felt so alive yesterday, so close and connected. But now…

In her room she picks up the Video8 cassette tape. Only this and the more dismayed than normal bedsheets stand as testament that anything at all had happened last night. They don't own anything to play this tape. Adrastos brought an old TV from his grandparents, but neither of them had brought a cassette player when they moved in. Not like they can afford one.

It hits her. The neighbors. Franklin. He has like a dozen cassette players.

Eddy quickly puts on more presentable pants and goes next door. The sky is all clouds and hovering water just waiting to burst. Eddy knocks.

A minute passes. She wants to knock again, but she hesitates. Why is no one answering? She knocks again.

Just as Eddy is about to turn away, she hears the lock *shh-clak*, and the door opens. Franklin looks out from the sliver of open space, the security chain perfectly blocking his eyes. He ducks a bit. "Oh, uh, Eddy, right? Hello. What do you need?"

He's wearing a bathrobe and slippers, his hair frumpled from sleep.

"Sorry. Did—did I wake you?"

"It is Saturday." He smiles a moment. "Just a second." He closes the door, the chain rattles, and then he reopens it fully.

Today's Saturday? "I guess I lost track of the week." Eddy looks away.

"It's fine. Don't worry 'bout it. I have cleaning and errands I should be doing besides sleeping anyway. So." He puts his hands on his hips. "Need a cup of sugar, neighbor?"

"No. No, actually"—a half smile ticks up on her lips—"I need a Video8 player."

Franklin's head pulls back a tad. "That's easy enough. Come back in like eight minutes, after I'm dressed, and you can use mine."

"Uh…I, um, well…I can't watch it here." She pushes the tips of her two pointer fingers together.

"Why not?"

"It's…personal," Eddy says softly.

Franklin's face remains skeptical for a moment too long, but then it brightens, his eyes opening wider as he grins. "Ah! Oh. Hmmm." He taps a finger on the side of his nose. "I know what it's like at your age." He pauses, grin lowering. "Not to say I'm old though! I mean, five, eight years ago, I remember that." The smile returns. "I can let you borrow it, but I need it back tomorrow."

Eddy nods. "Thanks. Thank you very much."

Half an hour later Franklin has left Eddy and Adrastos's apartment after helping her hook up all the cables. Really it only looked complicated. Now it's all set, the Video8 player resting on the floor with its tendril cables wrapped up and around the TV, ready to play the video.

Eddy sits on her legs on the carpet, staring at the cassette in her hands. She's excited. She's nervous. She has locked the door on the remote chance that Adrastos returns from work early; she will have at least some forewarning before they walk in. She's not going to do anything, but she really doesn't want them to see the video. Especially not Daryl. Slowly she slides the tape in and waits as it starts tracking.

Trees.

That's what the video starts on: trees. The person recording is walking through the forest, not doing anything in particular, just walking, the image bobbing up and down with the wind roughly whining in the background as it buffets the microphone. Eddy fast-forwards.

Lots of walking through the forest, then it cuts to walking down the town sidewalk. Philip focuses the shot on random cars, sometimes on an interesting window, until finally sitting down on a bench and filming people passing by on the opposite side of the street. The camera zooms in. The image still fairly clear. Eddy fast-forwards.

Philip is getting out of his car in the apartment parking lot. He walks toward their building. Halfway he suddenly whips the camera toward the forest nearby. He whispers something, and Eddy doesn't catch it. Philip turns back to the apartment building, but Eddy rewinds and turns the volume up.

"Stop calling me."

At least that's what she thinks he said. Eddy blinks, wondering about those words. As far as she knows, Philip doesn't have a pager, and he definitely doesn't have one of those new portable phones.

The video cuts to Eddy's dimly lit bedroom. The camera is pointed at Philip's chest and he sets it down on the desk. She sees herself on the bed. The image begins slipping up slowly, the frames not in sync. The bed rises as Philip's head is cropped off the top and reappears at the bottom of the screen. Eddy grunts, annoyed. Of course that would happen at this point on the tape, now, here. Of course. But as Philip leans down he becomes whole again, and she can ignore the slipping frames.

Only for a moment though. The whole image goes grainy and flickers out and then…oh gods. Oh gods and then! Eddy jumps back at what she sees, scrambling against the ground as she falls over to her side. A small wavering "aaaaaaah..." trickles out of her mouth; she is unable to scream.

The video keeps flipping and flickering, and fuzz covers the screen like mold, and there are three people in that room. "People" is too generous a word. The other being is—is—too tall. Too skinny. Too...inhuman! It's standing at the foot of Eddy's bed as Philip goes down on her. It has no face, it merely stands in a formal business suit wearing a black tie. No face at all. No eyes, no mouth, not even a raised feature for a nose. Its arms are too long, past its knees; its fingers are like white, dying vines.

It never moves. It never makes a sound, but the TV is now spitting out static along with her own moans crinkled up into a higher register, synthed out to unrecognition.

Eddy can't look away. Even as her breathing becomes too fast, too quick, unable to make any sound at all besides this panting. It doesn't end until she does in the recording, until Philip finally stands and clicks the camcorder off, and the whole time that thing is still there. Still, there! In her room. With them. Maybe even there right now.

The screen is black now, the TV silent. Nothing moves in the apartment. Nothing makes a sound until the tape finally runs out and pops up from the cassette player, and Eddy jumps, breaking her paralysis.

She moans and slumps sideways and can't think of a single thing to do, a single way to save herself. She's going to die, she knows it. She feels like she's freezing alive, and she knows it. She will turn to ice and melt into the floor and trickle into the earth and never exist again.

Her sides convulse, and she dry heaves onto the floor, small beads of saliva growing on her lips and slipping to the floor. Eddy is left with the rot of bile in her throat, and she cannot move.

The ceiling is bulging out again, like it always does, like she has always seen it do but never done anything about. Water is sloshing about in her body, and she dry heaves again, a blob of sickly green staining the carpet. Nothing can save her against the walls themselves, crushing in on her.

Eddy pushes herself to her knees and hands, and the floor is covered in moss, such soft moss she could sleep on it. But the apartment above her. The apartment above her is filling up with the ocean itself and it will crush her in mere moments if she doesn't run, doesn't escape. She flings the door open and runs up the stairs to the abode above. Eddy hammers the door with her fists, tears running down her face.

"Stop! Stop!" she screams. "Turn off the water!"

The door opens and of course, of course, it all makes sense. A man is standing in flippers and swimsuit, wearing a black scuba mask with a snorkel trailing seaweed from the top, and the whole apartment is filled with murky water. Murky water that does not escape even though the door is open. It's raining so hard outside anyway; the amount of water in the two places is almost equal.

The man glubs a few times, the last of his air expelled from his lungs, and reaches out to her, hand breaking the membrane where water meets air. Eddy screams and runs.

in silence,
befor , i am not going to tell
you

my silence, not con
tent
sistent
sent
my displacement thrugh you, us
them
the wolf at your throut,
FINGERS sinking ,,,,

you/me slash//me. don;t
down

he
"iwillnegateyourentireexistance"
- she made me say. she made me -
say. she made me say. Past made
me say. made me say. mother
made me say.

he " i have you "
he -

but he made me
lie down too

Splinter 20

Eddy sits bolt upright, still hyperventilating. The walls are no longer crushing her, and she has to do something. How can she possibly know where that thing is if only the camera can see it? The TV is still on, but the black screen illuminates nothing. Eddy runs through the apartment, turning on every light and shutting the blinds.

What if it's *here*?

She needs a camera. Even better, an instant camera. Under Eddy's mattress is her rent money. Not a lot, but surely enough. She takes all of it. She will figure out something later for rent and for that monthly DNA payment. That isn't important. Not now. She can only worry about these next few days. Later she can sell something…or something. Anything. Later. Right now, right now she needs to know where it is.

Eddy practically runs down the street, the light drizzle of rain clouding her eyes and hiding her tears. She keeps wiping her face, but it doesn't matter. At the pawn shop, she picks up the first instant camera she sees. They have a spare pack of self-developing film for it, and Eddy demands to know where she can find more. The man behind the counter is miffed but says the convenience store should have some.

Eddy runs to it, cradling her new instant camera in her arms, tucking it under her jacket to keep it from the rain.

Inside she finds the right aisle and takes every pack of film they have, spilling them across the checkout counter. A manager comes over and after Eddy apologizes several times in quick succession, she is able to buy the film, but she can only afford about a third of what she had grabbed.

Outside the store Eddy tears off the cellophane wrapping on one of the packs and loads up the camera. She spins around and snaps a shot. *Clik-clik, bzuuuu.* The camera spits out the square photo. Eddy has seen people use these before; she snatches it out and waves it in the air. Agonizingly slowly the image starts to fade in. Eddy flicks it faster through the air, keeping her head down and ignoring anyone around her.

Finally the shapes come into focus, even though the colors have not fully formed. Nothing she can't already see: the doors, the display inside, the trashcan. She's safe.

Eddy walks home. She has the pack of film loaded in the camera and the four packs in her shopping bag. That's fifty photos, minus the one she just used. She hopes it's enough.

She stops in front of her apartment building and takes one photo in all four directions. She holds the four white bordered images between her fingers like a hand of tarot cards, fanning them to force the development along faster.

Nothing.

Nothing.

Nothing.

…something?

In the photo facing away from the door there seems to be some black line in the background across the parking lot. Eddy looks up and doesn't see anything. At least, nothing that could have made that little black line. She looks again at the indistinct line deep in the background of the photo. *If only it weren't so small!* Eddy hurries into the apartment and locks the door.

An hour or two passes. Eddy has taken photos of every room in the apartment twice, burning through a second pack of film with the third already loaded in. Two more unopened.

Now she's sitting on the kitchen floor, back against the wall, eating peanut butter out of the jar. It's making her so thirsty, but she doesn't dare get up. The instant camera sits on the floor between her feet, and the dishwasher is gurgling away next to her. Eddy doesn't really know why she turned on the dishwasher. She guesses just for the sound of it, but there had been a few dishes in it.

Eddy waits. And waits. That video, that cassette, that thing on it. That's it. That's exactly what she needs. Concrete evidence. Hawthorn could reopen the diagnosis—and quickly, surely.

Finally the door lock is opened and someone enters. "Hey," they call out, "Harold sold more mattresses than normal today. Good news." The words are followed by a straw slurping. That must be Noah.

"Help." It's the only thing Eddy can think to say.

Noah comes around the corner holding a smoothie and sees Eddy sitting on the floor. "What happened? Where'd that camera come from?"

"I saw it."

Noah freezes. He swallows, then swallows again before asking, "W-what?"

"The thing. The thing in this place. It—it's on the video, but I can't *show* them." Eddy rolls her head back, squeezing her eyes shut. "I *can't*."

Noah's jaw is quivering. "What is it?" he whispers.

"I don't know!" Eddy digs her spoon into the peanut butter again, but the thought of putting it into her mouth is more repulsive than she can stomach. She drops the spoon, and it sticks to the floor. "Tall. Skinny. No face."

Noah has his eyes shut now. "I—I can't do this. I'm gonna—" Adrastos lowers their head a bit. "Fucking baby, gods dammit." They leave the smoothie on the counter and crouch down next to Eddy and put a hand against her cheek. "Okay. What the shit is happening? What the shit is attacking us?"

Eddy knows it's Daryl. He's so obvious sometimes. And his hand, his hand on her face, the tip of his middle finger gently pressing that little divot of her earlobe down like he always did.

"I dunno. I dunno," she moans. "But it's on the video, and I can't show anyone that video."

"Why?"

"*Because*. Please, Daryl."

"*Why*?"

"I…it shows, on it, Philip—he's…he's sucking me off. And you can see everything in the video."

Daryl just shakes his head. "As if I didn't know you'd be having sex with him eventually." He's silent a moment. "I don't care. I need to see what it is."

Eddy shivers. "Please. Please no."

"What are we gonna do otherwise?"

Eddy doesn't respond.

"Hmph." Daryl stands. "Where is it?"

Slowly, she raises a single hand. "There. In the cassette player. On the floor. I'm borrowing it. From the neighbors."

He leaves the kitchen without another word.

Eddy covers her face with her clammy hands and moans softly. She can't bear to look or listen or even acknowledge what Daryl is about to see. There's a minute of near silence as the Video8 player rewinds the cassette. The video starts.

Eddy hears someone's footsteps crunching through a forest.

Several moments pass, then Daryl asks, "Is this the right tape?"

Eddy nods and squeaks, "Yes."

The film is fast-forwarded. Over a minute goes by, and Eddy can't stand the whining of the tape as the reel spins spins spins, racing toward her mortifying moments captured there. Why did that part have to be when that thing showed up? *Why* did it have to show up at all?

The tape is played normally. Eddy hears Philip's voice, hears the bed creak, hears everything again, hears everything Daryl is watching.

"Holy shit," Daryl exclaims as the TV turns to static, and Eddy knows the image is flickering right along with the light flickering against the wall.

The apartment is devoid of movement and sound for a time. Eddy simply has to get through today. That's all she has to do. Just today. Just get through today.

Daryl returns to the kitchen, his hands shaking. "What…what is that? What is it?"

"I don't know." Eddy shakes her head quickly.

"We're fucked. We're so fucked. DNA didn't even see this!" He drops to his knees in front of Eddy. "Did you call them yet? What did they say!"

She mumbles something.

"What?"

"I haven't. I haven't called anyone."

"*Why*?" He grabs her shoulders. "We can't handle this!"

"I can't, I can't, I can't." Eddy shakes her head again, eyes closed, a few tears running down her cheeks.

"Call them! Give me the number!"

"I can't. It's me, and I'm there, and *it's me* on the screen. I can't. I can't show it. I can't have anyone see that. See me."

"Dammit, Eddy!" He shakes her. "I—I—I'll go! Right now!" Daryl stands.

Eddy grabs his wrist with both hands. "No, no, please," she moans. "I *can't*."

Daryl's hands are still shaking. Shaking harder. Eddy can't even keep his wrist still between both her palms. She's so cold and her mind is fracturing with headaches. If they were at her father's house, they could run down to the basement and huddle there forever and ever. Night has fallen, and they both know this as the frozen image of that tall thing wavers on the TV screen.

"I have to—" Daryl starts, "I have to—to protect Noah." But he begins coughing. And coughing. And coughing. He doubles over as the body's lungs rebel, and they sink to their knees.

Eddy can't support them as they fall. "Daryl!" She crawls a few inches closer and raises a hand, but she's coughing, too, and it stops her from fully reaching out, from touching them.

A few minutes pass, and Eddy is on her back now on the cold linoleum of the kitchen floor. She cranes her head backward and sees Adrastos standing upside down a few feet from her. Their hands are no longer shaking, but they sway slightly from side to side, as if drifting.

"Why…" they say slowly. "Why…I…I am, not here?"

"…w-what?"

"Here. Not. No." They shuffle toward the door.

"Wait." Eddy raises a hand and repeats louder, "Wait!"

"No, no. I can't. It hurts. It hurts." Their voice drifts across the apartment, floating away. The door is opened, the hinges squealing loudly.

"Adrastos!" Eddy rolls to her side, to her stomach; she forces herself up.

The living room is empty; the door is open. That thing is still glowing on the TV, its image flickering more now than before as the videocassette player begins to degrade in its projections.

Eddy stumbles forward, her legs not working correctly, not responding quite right, not moving fluidly. She leans against the arm of the couch and looks out into the blackness of the night. A slight drizzle is coming down, but she can only hear it, not see it. She has to stop them. She has to get her Adrastos back. Eddy leaves but catches herself at the door. She spares forty seconds to get the instant camera and her shoes and runs after them.

I will drift across these
more baren lands and I
will miss my entire life for
you. 'I will miss my entire lif
-e ror you.'
That is what you made me say. made me
do..
YOU drifting high/far above, but
not me. you. drifting high/far above.
High/fsr.. Forever without. High/far above.
avove. me..   I was nothing but.

nothing but, for all those calls
you led me on, all those hands y
ou let on me.. ALL those.those. ?
noy me. Displaced displeasure di
smember. ME. me. its me, now, it
why now, gone now, gone now, hig
h/fsr away. away. nothing but.nothing
but

nothingnothingnothingnothingnothing
nothingnothingnothingnothingnothing
nothingnothingnothingnothingnothing
nothingnothingnothingnothingnothing
nothingnothingnothingnothingnothingnothingnothin
nothingnothingnothingnothingnothingnothingnothin
nothingnothingnothingnothingnothingnothingnothin
nothingnothingnothingnothingnothingnothingnothin
nothingnothingnothingnothingnothingnothingnothin
nothingnothingnothingnothingnothingnothingnothin
nothingnothingnothingnothingnothingnothingnothin
nothingnothingnothingnothingnothingnothing nothi
nothingnothingothingniothimgnothingnothingnothin
nothingnothingnothingno hingnoyhningnnithningthn
nothingnothingnothingnothingonhtnhonthihgnothing
niothingnothingnoihth onhtnthinhgtihgnothingnoth
nothingnothingnouthingontihngonohtiugn thinotihg
nothingnothinthnonotoninhg ntioontoinhgontnoithi
nothingnothingtijonhthnoinnothingnothingnothijng
nothinnotignnthigntn thigntnoitnhotnnothigntnnot
npthongnotignnotingnotingnotingotnhitngnotihnton

Splinter 21

The night only holds wet darkness for Eddy. She can barely see, and the ground is sucking at her feet. Drops keep hitting her eyes, forcing her to blink. Her foot catches on a root, and she hits the ground, holding up the camera to save it from impact. Mud covers her front, seeping into her shoes and between her fingers.

Where is Adrastos? Where is she, for that matter? The forest is so close, so dense. The trees are like walls around her, the canopy a cacophony of twigs snapping and twisting around her. There is no moon, no stars, no light at all. Eddy snaps a wild picture in front of her. *Clik-clik, bzuuuu.* The flash showing nothing but trees and branches. The picture falls from the camera and is lost to the mud before she can catch it. She keeps running.

Eddy thinks she is going the right direction. But no, it's not really a thought. It's a feeling. Like a subtle current underwater sucking her forward. Branches and underbrush keep snagging like fingers on her arms and legs, but she ignores them. They're getting denser. One snatches away her camera, and Eddy panics.

"No!" she screams out as she half spins around, breaking the thin branch entangled with the camera strap. They can't have that! Can't have her protection and guide! Eddy cradles it in her arms against her chest and plows forward. If she can just run faster, just get there faster, nothing bad will happen. Nothing bad will happen at all. Just a little faster.

Eddy falls forward, the earth gone beneath her. She tumbles down a small decline and splatters across water. Again she desperately holds the camera aloft, accidentally flashing another picture as she clutches at the device.

Clik-clik, bzuuuu.

The light illuminates the spiraling limbs of wood above her, and the picture flutters down onto her wet face. She's in some small creek and soaked through to the skin. As she tries to stand, her hand and feet disappear into the slopping soil beneath her. Eddy wrenches her hand free with a sucking pop and crawls out from the basin of flowing water.

She keeps crawling, one hand hopping forward as the other holds up the camera. The trees seem to be clearing out slightly, ever so slightly, and Eddy looks up. A crumbling building stands across a small clearing that's slowly being overgrown by small saplings and weeds. Eddy has no idea what this place once was, but it doesn't matter now. She forces herself up and walks forward, her legs heavy with mud and water.

A distant flash of lightning gives her a quick view of the place: windows all busted, no standing doors, walls flaking and graffitied over countless times with now-fading paint. Eddy shuffles toward the closest door and stands before the opening.

The waiting at the threshold feels almost unnecessary. As if it's only by some propriety or tradition that Eddy must wait a moment before entering. Her entering is, after all, inevitable.

"Adrastos!" she calls out as she steps into the ancient structure.

Everything is rather quiet: only a slight pattering of rain can be heard now. Eddy's footsteps are slow. The building is protected from the rain, but she feels no less wet nor cold than when she was outside. Her foot stumbles over something, and she almost falls as the few loose items tinkle away. She flashes a picture.

Clik-clik, bzuuuu.

Hollow beer bottles.

Eddy immediately wishes she hadn't taken the photo. Her eyes had been adjusting somewhat to the dim light, but now her world is pure shadow again.

She barks out, "*Adrastos*!"

A sound attracts her attention. Almost like a voice humming or whispering. Eddy proceeds toward it, sliding her feet along the ground with one arm waving out in front of her. She feels oddly unafraid.

She turns down a hallway and sees it's slightly brighter at the end. Hardly a noticeable difference at all, but perceivable if she turns her head just a bit to the side. Slowly, delicately, Eddy approaches.

The hallway ends at a large room with several windows along the opposite wall. There are some benches lined up on either side, all facing forward as if this were some sort of chapel. And Adrastos is here.

They're sitting on the floor near the middle of the room just in front of a raised section of floor against the far wall. In the slight light Eddy can see them, with their knees against their chest, gently rocking back and forth.

"A-Adrastos?" Eddy whispers.

"No. Not them." They don't look up.

"Who? Blank?" Eddy raises her voice slightly.

"You call me that." He keeps rocking.

"Who are you?" She takes a set forward.

"Blank."

Eddy opens her mouth but hesitates a moment. "I don't—I don't know what that means."

"Me either. I thought it meant me, but I don't know."

"Where'd you come from?"

"Not here. Nowhere."

Eddy takes two more steps forward.

"Oh," Blank says quickly. "Noah wanted me to tell you. He's been thinking, and we've been talking. He wanted me to say, we're the unsaved. The unredeemed. The soulless, and the broken. There's no hope for us. That's what he said. He told me. I don't understand it. I don't understand anything. He also says, right now, that he thinks he finally realized it. Finally realized. Emptiness here has always been just another word for darkness."

"What are you talking about? 'We' who? You all? Adrastos?"

"I am not Adrastos. They do not claim me. And 'we' everyone. You. Me. Them. Us. All of us together. I'm coming together now."

"When have you been talking to Noah?"

"Always." Blank is shivering now as he keeps rocking.

"No…no way. He would've said something about it."

"He said no one would like me. That I have to be quiet. That I will not fit in."

Eddy can't bring herself to take another step forward. "No. Adrastos—them—they don't operate like that. Blank, I need you to get up. Come here. We have to go home."

"But I *can't*," he moans. "I don't know how. I don't know how I got here. I don't know. I don't know. My thoughts are all tangled up like dowsing rods over many under flowing rivers. But it's here. I'm here. Here. And I think, I think, this is…how to get home. Inside. Maybe? This thing, rocking? In front of me. I…I means me, right? I." Blank nods. "*Eye.*" He's shaking so violently now.

Eddy's lungs instantly feel frozen, and she gasps for air once, twice, again. And again. Her muscles finally expand, and she falls forward on her knees, coughing. Eddy's mind is swimming, scattered across thoughts of house and home. The apartment, her things jumbling in boxes in a van, her father. He's sitting at the kitchen table in their house in the city on the state border south of here. There are beer bottles lined up in an empty row in front of him as he clutches a crumpled photo of Mother in his hands.

"Mamá!" Eddy screams, tears on her face and a small line of spit hanging from her lip. The vision will not leave her eyes. She's tiny again and peeking into a kitchen she cannot unsee. She is sitting on her legs on the carpet just outside the kitchen door and she's cold and uncomfortable. Slowly, her father turns his head toward her.

"No!" Eddy jerks the camera up. *Clik-clik, bzuuuu.*

The camera flashes like lightning: a mere moment of clarity. Everything becomes black shadow again, night vision gone, and Blank is screaming. Really screaming. Like he's dying.

"Blank!" Eddy keeps pressing the button as fast as she can.

Clik-clik, bzuuuu. Blank is being lifted by something, lifted off his feet.

Clik-clik, bzuuuu. His hands are raised in front of him, holding something.

Clik-clik, bzuuuu. His face is covered in blood.

Clik-clik, bzuuuu. Their eye sockets are being smashed in by something invisible, turning the two spheres into pulp, leaving only hollow gore behind.

The button will not press down anymore. Eddy crumples the spat-out photos in her hand, and she runs. She runs even as Adrastos keeps screaming. Blind in the night and crippling forest, Eddy staggers through mud and clinging underbrush, her feet crushing mushrooms, and her hair collecting leaves.

It could be behind her right now, and she has no way to know. The camera has run dry, and Eddy can only run terrified with a held breath of desperate hope to survive. She's thinking of nothing—just running and scrambling, almost on autopilot, but she's not strong enough to match the forest. The mud's too thick, the rain too strong. She's sinking and sinking and being sucked down into the earth itself. Up to her knees, her waist.

Eddy grabs a sapling, trying to pull herself up, but it's too young, and the small tree breaks, leaving her with nothing to grasp onto. She keeps sinking. She thinks she should be more afraid, but she hopes this will at least save her from that tall thing with the empty face. In a last effort to save the camera—it's value equal to eviction—she holds it above her head and holds her breath before her face submerges into the mud.

And she keeps sinking.

Farther.

Down.

Eddy's feet never touch anything solid, and she knows she is still descending. Her lungs begin burning with a cold fire, and she can't hold them much longer. Now she panics. Eddy flails her arms—at least as much as she can in the mud—trying to swim up or to the side, hoping to find solid ground or maybe a root she can pull up on. But there's nothing besides the crushing density around her, slightly warm. Then her foot feels cold.

Not just normal cold—cold air.

This sensation grows along her limb, up to her shin and knee, and now her other leg is feeling it too. It rises to her waist, and Eddy's toe touches something solid. She is standing as the rest of her body keeps sinking down. Eddy tries to swim down, her eyes bulging under her closed eyelids. Her midriff comes free of the mud, pulling up her shirt, making her stomach shiver against the cold air. It must be air.

Eddy falls free. She lands in a heap on a carpeted floor and merely lies there gasping and spitting out mud. The camera falls from her hands, and she wipes her face clear.

The apartment.

"No…" She groans weakly.

Eddy rolls to her back, mud oozing off her and seeping into the carpet. She's on the living room floor, and she simply assumes she must be dead.

Expanse Four

Splinter 22

A few hours later, or maybe a day later, Eddy is sitting naked on the floor in Adrastos's room, leaning against their bed. She left all the muddy clothes in the living room and took the rest of the photo packets. There are pages and pages of garbled text scattered around her along with dozens of instant photos.

She can't understand these pages, can't find any sense within them. Who in Adrastos wrote them? She had found them stacked on the floor next to the typewriter and dropped each one after reading it. They did nothing to help. The twisted words had only made her more afraid, and now she is periodically flashing photos at the open doorway, watching for that thing. Every image keeps coming up empty.

No one is here.

In the crumpled instant photos from last night, the tall thing is clear as can be, plainly set for anyone to see. Its fingers are like tentacles splaying out, too many from its hands. Its arms remain at the same half-raised position in each photo as the engulfing tangles lift Blank and eventually plunge into his eyes; the gore inside his skull hidden by these fingers in the photo.

Eddy has not stopped crying. A soft, long cry, marked only by her intermittent sobs and shuddering breaths. She has everything she could ever possibly need now. Photos and video of this monster that killed Adrastos. DNA can't say no.

Eddy slams her fist against the floor. "Damn you!"

She rolls her head back again and sobs. *Why? If DNA had tried a little harder. If Hawthorn hadn't given up.* Eddy clenches her fingers into her palms and presses the heels of her hands against her temples. *They let this happen. DNA, Hawthorn, that old crone at the help desk—all of them!*

"Damn it!" she yells again between tight teeth.

She has to call them. She has to—to do something. Something!

Adrastos is dead.

Eddy loads the last pack of photos into the camera and staggers to her feet. She's so glad the camera still works. She takes a picture of the door before leaving and a picture of the living room before entering.

Standing in the living room she notices a pile of muddy clothes near the door and wonders vaguely what they are doing there, but she ignores them for now. She still has the note with Hawthorn's pager number.

The line rings a few times after dialing the number and then it picks up to four quick beeps signaling the call connected. Eddy punches in the landline for the apartment as the callback number and hangs up. What now?

It could be hours, or even days, before Hawthorn calls back. She will have to show him the pictures. The video. Eddy covers her face with her hands and heaves a deep breath. *I can get through this. I just have to get through today. Just simply today. We'll work everything else out after that.*

She gets earplugs and showers, listening to the pretend worms in her hair. She checks the phone for voice messages, then dresses and checks again. Nothing.

Eddy stuffs a few of the photos of the empty apartment into her pocket, then turns to the muddy clothes still by the doorway. She bundles up the various pieces between her hands, keeping her arms extended. She dumps them into the bathtub and stares down at them a moment. Vaguely she can recall falling into a mud puddle, but she cannot remember any details beyond that. She'll deal with cleaning them later.

Right after that she checks voice-mail again, there is one unheard message. Eddy's heart picks up, and she holds her breath as she sets it to speakerphone.

"Hey, Eddy, it's Philip. Um, I wanted to see about getting together again to do something. We could do something cheesy like a movie date, or if you're working a lot of night shifts this week, then we could probably do something during the day. Like maybe lunch and walking in the park. Up to you." He's silent a moment. "So yeah. Just give me a call back. I'm looking forward to seeing you again. Bye!" The message ends with a loud clack of plastic on plastic.

Eddy doesn't move.

"Philip," she whispers.

She wants to call him. She really does. But she can't bring herself to. Eddy feels, dirty. Cursed. Dangerous. Like all those death chips are about to be cashed in and turned into a rolling tide ready to flatten her life. She cannot. She will not. *Adrastos isn't dead! He* can't *be dead.*

Eddy covers her ears and turns toward the doorway. She will find them. She will go back to that abandoned building, and she will find Adrastos asleep and lost because Blank is still fronting, and he doesn't know where to go in this world. Eddy grabs her keys, locks the door, and sets off before her mind can fully think through what she is doing.

Outside is overcast and lightly misting this morning. Not a proper rain, but some water is falling from the sky regardless. Eddy shivers but won't go back. She will only be gone an hour or two. She tells herself this and clenches her teeth. *I'll be gone such a short time, I won't need a sweater!*

She enters the forest.

Eddy has no idea where that abandoned building is, but she doesn't let that fact stop her. She has the instant camera around her neck even though she doesn't remember having grabbed it. Almost instinctively she raises it to her eye and snaps a photo.

Clik-clik, bzuuuu.

She flicks it in her fingers as she continues walking, not waiting for it to develop. Shortly the image fades in, but it holds nothing besides the forest already around her. Eddy presses on, assuming she will find the place without knowing its location. She will follow the mud and broken branches. That will work.

A while passes. Longer than Eddy thinks it should take to reach her destination. She blindly believes she is still going the right way, but she feels like she should have run into it by now. The journey last night hadn't taken this long, even accounting for her running. Then she notices a small square of white on the forest floor.

Eddy dashes over to it, veering off course slightly. The photo is water damaged, but it still shows the forest in darkness. It's one of the images she had taken last night. She stuffs the photo into her pocket with the others and continues on, reaffirmed of her correct course.

Eventually she comes to a swiftly running creek and she remembers this, too, remembers falling into it. She's almost there. After jumping over it she still walks farther. Half an hour maybe. Maybe a little longer. Eddy's not sure. The sun is behind the clouds, and this abandoned building feels so, so faraway now.

She finds another forgotten photo that still only shows the forest in darkness. She pockets it and continues. And continues.

The trees begin to clear, and Eddy finds it. The abandoned building crumbling in the middle of the forest. And she feels nothing. There's no sense of finality about reaching this place. No fear. No guilt. Nothing. It's just a building.

Inside there are flakes pulling up and peeling from the yellowing walls. Dirt and broken bottles linger over the floor. Eddy retraces her steps with ease in the bright building, picking her way through the silent halls. She finds that room.

The big room, the one in the center of the building. The room where Adrastos…

Eddy holds her breath as she takes a step inside. The walls are faraway, and directly before her is an aisle between two rows of pews. It ends at a raised platform with an altar on it and a broken stained-glass window of three interlocking triangles.

Adrastos isn't here. Neither them nor their body. Eddy's feet begin shuffling forward—tentatively, but still forward—even without her fully commanding them. Between the raised altar and the first row of pews is a symbol drawn in the dirt: a circle with an X through it. It's at the same spot where Adrastos had been sitting, but there's simply no trace of them at all. No other scuffs or traces in the dirt. Not even footprints.

She raises the camera for a photo, but the button will not click down. It's spent. All out of juice at the epicenter of the disorder. Eddy doesn't lower the camera. She doesn't move. It's like she has hit a wall so solid it absorbs the entirety of her momentum.

After standing for several minutes Eddy simply decides that she hadn't wanted to move. Instead she is a statue at the bottom of the ocean, collecting coral and seaweed that create new rough coverings over her entire body like a second skin of rock. Sea stars and lobsters crawl across her and, she is blind to everything beyond the small radius of murky water around her.

Finally Eddy reaches back with one hand, attempting to locate the pew behind her without looking. She flails once or twice; she then finds the armrest and guides her body down. Adrastos is gone, and there's nothing she can do.

She sits long enough to notice the dull beam of sunlight shift across the floor during the intermittent moments when the clouds break. Two black ravens alight on the broken ledge of the stained-glass window. The camera sits on the ancient wooden pew right beside her, rather useless without anything to fill it. Eddy doesn't want to stay. Eddy doesn't want to leave.

"Oi. You got some change?"

Eddy jumps in her seat and turns around, gripping the pew's back. A middle-aged man is sitting in the very last row behind her. He's wearing a dirty blue beanie over long blond hair that hides his left eye. He has a rather full beard, too, and a walking stick leans against the front of his shoulder.

"Did ya hear me?" he asks, his voice rough.

"W-who are you? Why are you here?"

"Me? I'm just a wanderer. And why are you here?"

"I…I dunno."

"These days, these days…" The man shakes his head and grumbles something more.

"What?"

"Nothin'. Never ya mind." He stands, leaning on his walking stick heavily. He's wearing a blue windbreaker and also has a duffel bag resting at his hip, the cord strapped over his shoulder. "You draw that there?" He gestures with his chin at the circle with an X.

"No. Not me. I found it."

The man hobbles toward her, not bothering to brush the hair from the side of his face. "Then, tell me, what are ya gonna do about it then?"

"Do about what?"

"All of it, you fool." He waves the walking stick up, then leans on it again. "Just sittin' there won't do nothin', and you not givin' me any change won't do nothin' neither."

"But I don't have…" Eddy's eyes fall to the camera beside her. "I, well, I have this." She holds it up to him.

The wanderer chuckles. "Mm, mmm." He holds the staff in the crook of his elbow as he considers the token. He puts it in his duffel bag. "Yes. Good. I can maybe tell ya somethin' now."

"Wait, you're just gonna *take* it?" Eddy leans forward and is about to jump up after it, but she loses the moment and can't muster the energy anymore.

"Ya gave it to me, didn't ya?"

"But…"

"Ha! Then do ya want it back?" He lifts it partway from the bag. "Or do ya want to trade for somethin' better? Hm?"

"Better? What are you even talking about?" Eddy stands up now.

" 'Better' as in where ya need to go if you're after that." He points to the symbol on the floor.

"How would you know?"

"I've seen some things while wandering these parts. Heard some things, too." He taps the side of his head and smirks.

Dozens of thoughts wash through Eddy's mind. She has to go home to fix things, get her life sorted out. She probably doesn't have a job anymore; she definitely doesn't have money for rent anymore, or for that fine. Adrastos is…gone. What does she really have left now? What pieces even remain to be put back together? Philip? She hadn't called him back. But what can she offer him if she has nothing herself?

"Ya got revenge, and ya got penance. Which one are ya gonna follow?"

"What? I don't…that doesn't even—" Eddy shakes her head. "What are you talking about?"

"Take ya camera and go home. Ya not committed to this." He holds it out to her.

"No." She pushes it back toward him. "If Adrastos is still alive, I'm gonna save them!"

"Ya can't do both. Keep that in mind. You can't be empty and full at the same time."

"Shut up. I don't even know what you're talking about. I'm gonna go find them. There's no body. There isn't even blood! They have to still be alive."

The wanderer just *tsks* with his lips. "No turning back from here, mind you."

"I don't care. Where do I need to go?"

The wanderer is silent a moment. He stuffs the instant camera back into his duffel bag and points to a side doorway. "Through there, turn right. Walk out as straight as ya can through the woods. There'll be a path soon enough. Head left this time and keep going till ya see an old house. That's where ya wanna be."

"That's it?"

"That's it."

Eddy nods slightly, then turns toward the doorway. Before she leaves the small chapel, the man calls out to her.

"Mind the orison. You should keep those words on your lips, girl."

She turns around. "How did—?" But he's gone. The chapel is empty, and the wanderer is nowhere to be seen.

Eddy shivers and grits her teeth. "Stupid old man," she mutters.

She leaves the ancient building and treks through the damp forest again. She knows the goodly orisons—well, at least the main one. The main one is the most important anyway. Her mother taught it to her so many years ago.

Eddy stops walking. It has been such a long time. She hadn't even realized before how the time has been passing. How the years just keep stretching and stretching between the present and that last time she had seen her mother. And that time will only keep getting longer, endlessly longer as the infinity of time continues to pass before her. Eddy feels a tear sliding down her face as she sniffs. She isn't going to cry now. She won't let herself.

Instead she recites the goodly orison softly under her breath. "Circled by the goodly charms, cradled by the strongest arms. Shielded by the brightest light, sheltered by the hidden might."

Eddy keeps whispering the small reassurance to herself with every footfall in the otherwise silent forest. The countless trees stand congregated around her, but there's not a single being with ears to hear the anxious words. Shortly, Eddy finds the pathway and begins following it. Not after that, the outline of a house appears behind the trees.

Weeds are choking out my lungs spewing
vapors. Tangled betweem trees
I hang dying. Dead. Ev en these
are food for some, others.
Do you thinkme dangerous? Wrong?
A mossenger from forgotte. n
I am broekn with out flesh
feelings, more, or so.
I have moss covered
teeth and lichen
tangled eyes.

My future is stamped out on tarot
cards, bent and over-used. Bent
over and never returned, worse than
a dog-eared page. I am composit of dust
before water logged leafs. I am for
grasping but not for you. I won;t.
I won't.
won t
wan t
re
sulute. you.....
but
? /help/ you

I will slink through
these hollow places
and find a home no
one else could want.

Splinter 23

This house is almost a mansion. Two stories, expansive, a few windows broken out. Several of the shutters hang only by a single hinge, and the paint has long ago faded out. There's no graffiti on the outside, though. A spacious porch stretches across the front of the house.

Eddy slowly ascends the four steps. There's dirt and some leaves across the wooden patio; a few planks are broken too. The front double doors are open a crack and there's no goodly charm. Eddy gently presses a hand against the door, but it doesn't budge. She pushes harder, but the frame is warped, and the bottom of the door is stuck to the ground. Using her shoulder as well, the door finally comes free with a loud groan of wood and scraping on the floor, and Eddy stumbles into the house.

There's no furniture. Nothing on the walls. A rotting rug crumpled on the floor is the only distinguishing feature in the entry hall, aside from the layers of dust on the walls and more dirt and scattered leaves on the floor.

Slowly, Eddy begins picking her way through the ancient building, clutching the goodly charm through her shirt as she goes. Like a ghost, she searches through the house, keeping close to the walls to avoid creaking the floorboards. There's a broken chair in one room. A few broken beer bottles in another. The kitchen is entirely empty, no refrigerator or dishwasher. Even the drawers have been taken out of the counters, every last one. There's no door to the pantry, and the shelves stand with only cobwebs and dead insects.

Beyond that, nothing.

Eddy returns to the entry hall and looks up the stairs to the darker second floor. The stairs look okay. Can they still support her? Eddy tests a foot on the first step, and it creaks loudly. She freezes, then lifts her foot away. Maybe if she hugged the wall as she climbed, she'd be fine. But she's rather hesitant to test that.

Eddy walks down the hallway, attempting to examine the safety of these stairs. Underneath the stairs is more wall, so she can't tell where she would fall into if they did collapse under her. Probably just a closet.

At the end of the hall and to the right, Eddy finds a doorway that leads directly under the staircase. This one sticks too at first, but it comes open easily once it's free from the frame. There's not much she can see, and the lack of light in the middle of the house isn't helping her search. The ceiling of the closet is slanted to accommodate the stairs, and the room ends only about four feet in. But on the opposite wall, there seems to be something on it. Eddy leans forward slightly, and something long hanging from the ceiling brushes across her face.

She yelps and jumps backward, falling to the floor. Eddy clutches a hand over her chest and tries to catch her breath before standing. She can't see anything inside the closet that could have touched her.

Once back on her feet, Eddy studies the dimly lit space again. Now she sees it. A pull cord. She sighs and chuckles a bit at herself. She might as well try it.

The closet fills with light from a 20-watt bulb, balancing the darkness, and there *is* something on the opposite wall. Three wheels carved into the wood, each segmented into numerous individual sections with small pictures or symbols in them. The small center circle created by the inner wheel has a square within it. There seem to be slight hairline gaps between each wheel.

Eddy blinks twice in surprise. "What?"

She turns and walks a few steps away from it. For a moment she just stands, her breath shallow, hands shaking slightly at her sides. *This can't be.* Eddy glances over her shoulder, confirming the thing in the wall is really there.

Eddy walks slowly back into the closet. If these wheels are just carvings, then that's it. She can go home, and it's all over. She will get Hawthorn and call Philip, and the police will find Adrastos, and everything will go back to normal. But she already knows what this carving is. There's a small arrow at the top of the carving, and ever so slowly Eddy touches the outer wheel with a trembling hand and it rotates.

"No," she whimpers. "No. Why?"

Eddy turns from it again, hands over her face. *Is this really happening? Some monster is hunting us, Adrastos gone, and now this! This—this spinning puzzle!* Eddy shuffles away from the closet and back into the hallway, where she leans against the wall and starts hyperventilating. She slumps to the floor, tears on her palms.

"I'm gonna kill you," Eddy mutters into her hands. She punches the floor. "I will fucking murder you."

With a focused effort, she gains control of her lungs again and pushes herself up from the floor. She shuffles slowly back into the closet, wondering if she can break this seal open and unleash its secrets. It's just wood. Just planks nailed up against more planks, standing off the ground to make the house's skeleton. All that empty space between the walls of this building, empty spaces where no one has ever been. Anything could be inside them.

If she just had a crowbar, or a sledgehammer. Even a wrench. That would do the trick. Eddy considers this destruction as her eyes continue to float over the various carved pictograms. She gasps.

Right there, near the bottom of the outer wheel, is a face. An empty face without any features or markings at all. She almost overlooked it, almost thought it was just an omega and looked away. But that's it. Eddy knows it. That's the face of the thing that's after them. There's nothing else in the outer wheel with significance even close to this image. So what else can she do, except rotate it to the top?

As each image from the outer wheel passes the small arrow at the top, the puzzle makes a slight *click* behind the wall. Eddy still can't believe this is happening.

The middle wheel has little of interest to her, nothing that immediately jumps out at Eddy, until she sees the tentacles. A torso with arms that end in an expanding web. The puzzle is building that thing, building up its image like some disassembled shrine.

"Dammit. *Why*?" Eddy mutters. She hesitates but spins the image to the top of the middle wheel. She glances over her shoulder. Still an empty house.

The inner wheel is mostly planetary symbols, same as the icons on the bottom corners of her tarot cards. But the only choice—clear as can be, like a body still breathing in a morgue—is the circle with an X through it, the same symbol traced into the floor of the chapel. Eddy closes her eyes, hands trembling, and spins the inner wheel into place.

Nothing happens.

Eddy looks behind her again and then looks to the center circle with a square within it. She reaches up to press it, but her hand freezes before touching the wood. She is preparing herself. She is being silent to hear if anyone is in the house. She is waiting. She can't.

She can't push her hand forward.

Not now. Please…not now. I'm just—I'm just being careful. Stupidly careful. I don't have to keep waiting. Press it. Press it. Dammit, press it.

The first time Eddy ever remembers this happening was back in grade school. A test was laid out in front of her, and she readied her pencil but left it hovering over the paper. She had told herself she was thinking, preparing, making sure she remembered everything, but she knew the answer to the first question. And the second. To all of them. But half the allotted time passed by without her hand or any part of her body moving at all. She had failed that test because too many questions had been left unanswered at the end.

Finally her hand pushes through the air as if through icy water, slowly reaching the wood until the tip of her middle finger brushes the surface, and she can move again. Eddy is ready, after preparing herself and making sure no one is behind this wall, Eddy presses down on the center circle.

It resists at first, but she presses harder. With a quick series of clicks, the wall comes loose and swings slightly inward out of its frame. Beyond is darkness.

Eddy swallows. "Anubis preserve me." She gives it another push, and the wall is open completely.

Stairs lead downward; the closet light only reaches as far as the bend about eight steps below. This is not an answer.

That old man lied to her. Eddy grits her teeth and takes a tentative step down. The stairs are stone, and everything is completely silent.

Eddy peeks around the corner at the bend. Another eight or so steps continue the descent, ending in a large, mostly dark room. A single hanging light illuminates one of the far corners, and a few tables are pressed up against the walls. There's a door in the far corner as well. Besides those things, nothing else draws Eddy's attention.

The basement floor is cement, and in the half light there seem to be drawings scrawled across the ground in the open center of the room. As Eddy walks across this empty space she is focused on the floor, trying to make sense of the large circles and lines spread out around her.

Klunk. Eddy's vision blurs, and black dots pop in the center of her eyes. She staggers forward and falls to her hands and knees. The room is spinning, and her head is in more pain than ever before. She vomits up bile and can't even think.

Klunk. She falls flat from the second blow, vision tunneled, everything jittery and out of focus, and everything everything hurts. The world goes dark.

Eddy opens her eyes. Is she being pulled? Darkness again.

Eddy wakes once more, and everything is too bright as if the sun itself has been crammed into the ceiling above her. She's on her side, knees pulled up to her chest, and she tries to reach out, but her fingers jam against metal bars. Someone is speaking, but the sound is muffled, not that Eddy could focus on the words if she wanted to. The pain is a spike drilling down her skull, into her spine, ready to reach into her guts and stir them up like a reverse blender. She feels too hot, and she feels too cold.

"Adrawss…" She slurs the name and can't even finish it. She doesn't know where she is or where she was or what she is doing. She thinks Adrastos is digging up a basement in the apartment, digging up a well, like in that movie. The landlord will cut off their paint if they don't stop. All Eddy wants is for that camera to get unstuck from her hand.

eye

i belong in no place,
so i can go
into any place
and still not belong there

still not
belong t here

..

Splinter 24

Eddy wakes up in a comfortable bed in a room she is unfamiliar with. Her head is wrapped with bandages, and instead of her clothes, she's wearing foreign flannel pajamas that smell like old cedar. She starts to push herself up, but an immediate wave of dizziness and subtle nausea forces her back down. On the wall across from the bed, there is a painting of an older woman. The ceiling is a pattern of squares edged in wood, old and warping around the edges and at the corners of the room. Something beyond the ceiling is groaning out a perpetual sound that slinks back and forth behind the wooden tiles.

The springs of an ancient recliner squeak softly, and someone is in the room with her. Across from the foot of the bed, a man stands. A man too slender and too tall. His arms twig-like, fingers longer than his palms and bent at slight angles, his torso crooked slightly to the side. And though he has a face and graying hair, he is still far too similar to that monster coming after them.

"W-who! Who are you? What are you?" Eddy tries to crawl away, to push herself into the headboard as if to scamper down into the crevice between the bed and the wall, but she has nowhere to escape to.

"Calm down, son," the man says. "This is just a condition I bear."

"Who are you?" Eddy pulls the pillow around over her chest as if it could be a shield.

"I am Miles Randly Timberson, and I think you are exactly the person I need."

"W-what?"

"Do not fear. I understand you are confused." He sits on the bedside and Eddy tries still in vain to pull farther away from him. "I must apologize for my son. He's the one who clobbered you over the head twice. He gets a bit carried away. But you were intruding." Timberson rests a too long finger over his mouth. "You've never had any liver conditions, have you?"

"Conditions?"

"Liver conditions. Prior, or maybe in the family?"

"Uh…no."

"Good. Good. I patched you right up and gave you some acetaminophen. You had a concussion, that is. But don't worry. I work at a hospital."

"You—you're a doctor? Timberson?"

"*Mister* Timberson. Use the proper social cues, child." He reaches out to Eddy. "Your wrist. Hand it to me."

Eddy's mouth is agape slightly, and she just stares at him as if the lanky hand is an iron maiden.

"Come now." Mr. Timberson grabs Eddy's arm and wrenches it from the pillow. His fingers coil around her wrist and overlap by several inches. He looks down at his pocket watch and is silent for a minute, head bobbing a bit as he counts out Eddy's pulse.

Mr. Timberson finally releases Eddy's wrist. "Yes. Quite normal now. I think you will pull through just fine. The dizziness may continue, but not for much longer."

"Why is your hand like that?"

"Like what, son?"

"So long." Eddy is barely speaking above a whisper. "Your whole body. You're like that…thing."

"Yes. Yes." Mr. Timberson folds his hands in his lap, elbows sticking out, and nods as if Eddy has just recited some holy text. "Yggdrasil. That is the thing of which you speak. And you have seen it. We know you have seen it, otherwise you would not have been able to open that lock into the basement."

"Who made it? Why? What is that monster?"

"My father's father constructed that hidden passage, back when my family lived in that very house. The land was chosen with purpose, but indeed, the land was too strong there. It turned out to be a poor living space." He smiles, and it is terrible. The crescent opening of teeth looks too large for his narrow face. Eddy looks away. "This was compounded when the land became steeped in my family's blood. And from the ossuary, which even now still stands, though well sealed."

"But—but ossuaries are illegal."

"It was constructed before that law. Grandfathered in, both literally and metaphorically." Mr. Timberson grins again.

"So you've kidnapped me? Just because I saw that thing? That, what? Ink-brazil?"

"*Yggdrasil,* child. Do not profane its name." Mr. Timberson stands. "Yggdrasil is the promise passed down from father to son over the generations, the promise brought from the old home to these lands. We are the only true practitioners still. We follow the ancient stories, the tales first told by Snorri himself, the tales of the end of time and the world to come. Only through Yggdrasil will we find salvation from the freezing fires. And you, son, you are important for that very reason. Yggdrasil has revealed itself to you. You are the Caller of Yggdrasil."

Eddy just shakes her head softly from side to side, not even certain if she would rather be locked in a room with this Timberson or with that "Yggdrasil." She opens her mouth to speak, but only a broken syllable flops out. Eddy gasps and swallows and tries again. "No—no way. I…I'm, not, no…no."

"There is no denying the truth. Why else would you be here? How else would you have found us?"

"That man. That crazy blue-beanie guy sent me."

"Who?"

"That—that guy. I thought he was a hobo, but he sent me right *here.* Blond hair in his eyes, wearing lots of blue. He's one of yours."

Mr. Timberson shakes his head. "I do not know him. This sounds like simple providence to me."

"No." Eddy licks her lips. "I—I want to leave. I wanna go home."

Mr. Timberson's eyes furrow and his lips purse, but the dark expression is pushed away as he sits again, and pulls up a plaintive look. "Child, you do not understand." He folds both of his hands over Eddy's, fingers extending over them onto the bedsheet. "You *are* home now. This is where you belong. You will help complete my work. We will usher Yggdrasil's true form into this world and collect up all the poor souls cast out and forgotten, bring them into the fold of the Tenth Realm, the Sheltering Forest, and save them until the birth of the new, purer world.

"This shall come to pass with me at the helm. I will eat your sin and your sickness. I will devour your pain and your failures. I will save you from these things so you will no longer know torment. *That* is my family's work, stretching back generations. Do you understand?"

"…no. I—no." Eddy shakes her head and tries to pull her hand away, but Mr. Timberson holds it firm. "I don't understand anything you just said."

Mr. Timberson sighs. "Very well. Consider the world at large. How many people have everything they need?"

"Uh, I dunno. Probably not a lot."

"Who helps those people?"

What? I don't—don't understand—"

"Just *answer* the question."

"Well, well…doesn't the government? I mean, or organizations? I dunno. Like charity? Churches?"

"That last one is a good point, and—perhaps—the closest to what I mean. But in reality, no one truly helps those people. So many, many privileged could help them, but none of the privileged do. Countless individuals have no one to turn to. Countless people are poor and destitute. But I am here for them. I am here for everyone cast out. The gays. The gypsies. The psychotics. All of them I will bring into my embrace. All those who are thrown out and left over as scraps from society's high table. All of them will come to me and all will be eternally grateful for my bountiful generosity."

Again, Mr. Timberson's words flood over Eddy without any offer of purchase or help against the tide. She looks away at the ceiling, as if she could find some pocket of respite from his sermon. The groaning above them sounds more like a wheezing hiss now.

"What is the matter, child?" Mr. Timberson asks.

"I—I just can't handle this right now. I didn't even want to come here. I wanted to find that thing that ki—ki—took Adrastos, and I wanted to stop it. To…to, k—combat it." Her hands are shaking; her mouth feels too tight. "It took my friends."

"Are you saying Yggdrasil took someone already?"

"Yes! Adrastos. They were a system. They were six people. That thing, your *Yggdrasil…*" She looks down. "It killed them. Killed all of them. Ripped their eyes out."

Mr. Timberson leans back slightly. "Yggdrasil does not kill. He *cleanses.* And saves. You say they were multiple people? How do you mean? Some sort of psychosis? Split personality?"

"No! They were a system, and they were just fine. They were actual people, separate from the body, and all six of them *died.*"

"Ha!" Mr. Timberson chuckles. "That is simply impossible. You can't have more 'minds' without there being a split personality, and you can't have that disorder without it being diagnosed. Sounds like a teen fad. Some, 'role-play.' *That* is your answer right there! That is why Yggdrasil cast them low. Your friend's pretending makes true sufferers seem less legitimate. You would allow that friend to tear down what little acceptance psychotic people have, just so your friend can have his jollies? No. That will not stand in the next world."

"Then how can you say you're for everyone!"

"Name someone else." He crosses his arms.

"I don't—I don't really know anyone else…" *Will anyone even realize I've been kidnapped? Philip? He'll think I've abandoned him.* Eddy's skin tightens across her back.

Mr. Timberson sighs. "Name a type of person then."

"Uh, well, how about trans people?"

"Ugh." Mr. Timberson rolls his eyes. "Truly? That is what you ask? I am here concerned about legitimate problems! *Trans*sexuals don't have a problem. Their bodies are perfectly fine. You might have a woman who loves women, so be it. She's gay." He waves a hand. "She will be perfectly accepted with all the other gays. 'Transsexual' is an unnecessary piece of terminology."

"No. No, you have no idea. You couldn't save anyone even if you really wanted to." Eddy tries to stand, to fight past the dizzy spirals in her head, but Mr. Timberson grabs her elbow.

"You are in no state to leave this bed, child." He pulls her back to the center of the mattress. "I shall send Ms. Bosco up to you." Mr. Timberson leaves the room, locking the door behind him.

That doesn't stop Eddy from trying. She hobbles out of bed, a hand on the side of her head, and she holds her breath in an effort to avoid vomiting. The door is ancient Victorian style with decorative carvings and even a true keyhole Eddy can peek through. The hallway on the other side has a few boxes lining the walls with blankets piled over them and an overstuffed bookshelf just at the edge of view.

The woman in the painting seems to stare down at Eddy as she uses the bed frame to support herself and shuffle to the window. The frame is nailed shut from the outside. The lawn around the house is overgrown with grass, and farther away, trees gently cluster together at the edges of the forest. And nothing else.

Eddy is sitting on the bed again, head down in her hands, nausea rippling around the edges of her being. The door unlocks, and an overweight woman wearing a cooking apron enters holding a tray of food. A young man a few years Eddy's junior closes the door and stands before it: arms crossed, long black hair tangling over his eyes, frowning.

"Here you are, dearie," the woman says as she lays the tray on the nightstand next to Eddy. "Fresh mushroom soup and my hot, handmade potato bread to sop it up. A bit of hot ginger tea, too. Master Timberson said you still felt ill. Do you like mushrooms? They've all been picked within four miles of here." She beams.

Eddy turns her head up partway. "Why can't I leave?"

The woman covers her heart with one hand. "So sorry, dear, so sorry. Not my place. Master Timberson's orders. But now, come, let's not think on that, shall we? I'm

Verdandi, but you can just call me Verdi, okay? I brought young Master Timberson as well so he can give you a right proper apology. Isn't that so, young Timberson?"

"I guess." He doesn't make eye contact.

"Not polite, hitting people," Verdi says softly.

No one speaks after that. Eddy just groans and lies back against the pillows.

Verdi bunches up her apron in her hands. "Come now, make a proper apology. Introductions first. Young Master Foster Timberson—and you, dearie, Master Timberson actually sent me for this reason too. You didn't even have a wallet on you when we brought you home. Just some pictures in your pocket. What's your name?"

"Eddy."

"Good, good. Eddy, Foster, I'll leave you to it. No pipes for hitting in this room." She titters and shuffles out into the hallway.

Once alone, Foster says, "Gods, I hate her."

"Why the shit did you try to smash my head in?" Eddy's face is turned to the ceiling, eyes closed, massaging her temples. The groaning above is more subtle now, but two muffled clanks reverberate beyond the wood, and the groaning rises in pitch.

"I dunno." Footsteps as he walks to the window. "I didn't mean to."

"You hit me twice."

"Yeah. I don't know. I guess I got scared. I went down there to…be alone. To get away from this mansion."

"Your dad said something about that house being worse."

"Hmph."

Eddy opens her eyes. Foster is standing at the window, leaning heavily on the sill. A light rain has begun misting from the sky.

"Is—is this place safe?" Eddy asks. "From the spirits in the mist? Since we're so far from town. We're right in the middle of the forest."

"It's fine. We've got more than enough goodly charms. Under every window, on every door, every cardinal direction. Can't leave without them knowing."

"Then what's that sound? Above us? In the attic?"

"The water. The plumbing broke down in here two years ago, so my uncle Elwood and Verdi's brother, Anton, spent a whole week setting up a new plumbing system in the attic. They didn't have to jack up the manor's foundation that way."

"Is it always so loud?"

"Usually. Neither of them are plumbers."

"Oh." Eddy leans over and looks at the soup. It smells excellent, at least. "So…this place, I mean, your dad…he made this all sound like some kind of cult thing."

"Yeah."

"Is it?"

"Yeah."

"And you're…part of it?"

"By birthright, but I don't have Marfan syndrome, so I can't be a 'high father.' " Foster does air quotes. "I'm like a vestigial limb you can't hack off. All my father's disappointment with everything in the world distilled into a single point."

"Really?"

"Yeah."

"So, Marfan syndrome? That's why he's so long and skinny?"

"Yeah."

"And…that thing? Yggdrasil—?"

"Don't say the name. I've never seen a scrap of evidence for it. It isn't real. My dad's just…insane."

"I've seen it," Eddy whispers.

For a near minute Foster just stays at the window, unmoving. He turns and knocks the bread from the nightstand. "No, you *haven't*. My father thinks you're the Caller of that thing, so he'll make you be part of the ritual. We'll do it, nothing'll happen, and then you'll just be one more disappointment that's stuck living here forever until you die. Like Mom. Dad's mom, my mom." He curls his lip and jabs a finger at the painting watching over them. "She was lucky. Doesn't have to live with this. Now eat your damned soup. I'm leaving." He goes to the door and takes out the key from his pocket.

"Wait," Eddy says. "Don't—don't lock it. Please. I have to get out."

Foster stares at the key in his hand. "He gave me this key as a test," he mumbles. "I know it. It'll be the board for me if I don't keep you here." Foster shuts the door and the lock clicks home.

if i am
named.
i am not
named.

i am not here, heart, heed
heel
pushed down from behind,
down from
he with fingers, he with, it
with. photos dropped in ahat
and shaken crambled: me, eye, i
me,memontos,me, jattered.
shiftingthroughmy
myoblongheart
hetakesitlikeheowns
itlikehealwaysdid
butneverdidhewont
listentomysilence
scatteredscentsand
wholebeingstornapart
acrossthechestandEATEN
cleantothebone
beforeanyone
knewanother
/////////
wasintheroomtoo

Splinter 25

Several days of recovery pass. Today Eddy is taken down from her room and packed into the backseat of a small sedan between two other members of the family: both men not more than ten years her senior. They are to ensure she doesn't try to run. Foster sits in the front passenger seat, head propped up by an arm.

The car is on, a mild heat blowing out the fans. Everyone is silent as they wait for the others to finish loading an older, wheelchair-bound man into an SUV parked a short distance from the front of Timberson manor. Mr. Timberson and Verdi finish securing the chair into the back, then Verdi packs the ramp away.

"No one's told me where we're going yet," Eddy says softly. This is the first time she's seen Foster again and the first time she's seen any of these new faces.

Anton, the man sitting to Eddy's right, says, "We can't tell you. The elders decide what you need to know."

Foster blows air out between his lips, jetting up a strand of his bangs for a moment.

Anton gives Foster's seat a soft kick. "Show respect."

Foster doesn't reply.

A new older man with a cane walks up to the sedan and gets into the driver's seat.

"My Father," Elwood, the man on Eddy's left, says.

"Father Eustace," Anton says.

"Children. Foster. Caller," Father Eustace's voice rasps. "We are ready to return."

Eddy squirms in her seat involuntarily. She wishes they would all stop calling her Caller. They keep meaning it as short for the Caller of Yggdrasil, but her last name really is Caller, and it keeps sending shivers up her spine. Eddy has kept that bit of information about her last name strictly to herself. No point in encouraging these people.

Father Eustace touches the goodly charm hanging from the rearview mirror, then shifts the car into gear. They drive off, SUV first and their sedan following. This is the first time Eddy has been out of the manor since arriving, but there's little to see besides trees.

They bump along a gravel road through the forest. It's fairly well kept, as if it's traveled frequently, but after twenty minutes Eddy still hasn't seen anything like civilization. They must be very far away in the forest. Father Eustace turns down a different gravel road. The bumps are more jarring now, and there are more low-hanging branches that scrape over their heads like desperate tendrils. This road is much less kept. Much less traveled.

Even with the heat from the car's fans, Eddy feels cold. She tightens her arms around her chest and shivers.

"You feel it?" Elwood asks.

"Cold?" Eddy responds.

"No. His presence. Like walking through a cool mist. It tightens your skin and sharpens your focus." Elwood's voice drops in volume. "The old house is very strong with him."

"We're going, back there? To that basement?"

"Quiet," Father Eustace cuts in. "You are not a member of this family. You will not speak further."

Anton shakes his head.

They pull up to the house shortly after. Foster is sent over to help bring the wheelchair man out of the SUV, and Eddy remains flanked by Elwood and Anton even out of the car. She is given a small cooler to carry. Father Eustace walks slowly up to Eddy with the aid of his cane and stares at her a moment.

He shakes his head. "I won't believe you're the Caller until I see it. Come."

Up on the porch, Eddy looks back and sees the wheelchair man, but something seems off about him: his head listed to the side, long arms in an uneven fold in his lap. They place down a ramp over the stairs, he is wheeled up, and Eddy gasps.

"He's dead," she blurts out.

Skin all shriveled up against his bones, his jaw off-center, eyes shut. Mr. Timberson stops the chair in front of Eddy.

"This is my father. You will show him proper respect, child. Address him as Mr. Randly Silvester Timberson, and apologize."

"…w-what?"

"*Apologize.*"

Everyone stands silent around her, staring at her. Eddy's hands are so cold, and her heart is pounding now.

"Uh…uh, Mr. Randly Silvester Timberson, I—I apologize."

Mr. Timberson is silent a moment more, then says, "Very good. My father is still with us in all ways. My grandfather less so, because the ossuary is sealed, but they are both still vital members of the family. We enter."

A woman who rode in the SUV has a sleeping baby in a carrying carriage. Foster is carrying a small wooden box.

Inside the house they crowd around the door that leads under the stairs as Mr. Timberson enters the small space. The cooler starts feeling heavy in Eddy's arms.

As Mr. Timberson begins spinning the carved wheels, he recites, "Yggdrasil's avatar needs no Human senses. He transcends us. Yggdrasil's avatar is shaped as us, but his roots remain true. Yggdrasil's earthly seal is only but a glimmer of the truth passed down."

The door is opened, and Elwood and Anton carry dead Timberson in his wheelchair down the steps. Father Eustace locks a hand on Eddy's shoulder as she goes down the stairs ahead of him. Briefly she imagines jerking herself forward in some manner that would send Eustace tumbling down the stone steps, but she does not.

In the basement all the lights are on, and Eddy sees a great tree drawn out across the entire floor. The trunk is enormous, roots tangling all beneath it and branches reaching out partway up the walls. A table against the back wall has a wooden chalice and a wooden mallet, both inscribed with the circle and X.

"You know, I'm pretty sure everything in here goes against the new DNA codes," Eddy says.

"And why should we care about those new things? When our roots reach so much deeper?" Father Eustace replies.

Mr. Timberson directs everyone into positions around the tree. Foster sets the wooden box at a low point over the roots and leaves it there. The carriage with the baby still asleep stays next to the woman in the formation. Mr. Timberson takes the cooler from Eddy and places it near the table. From within he extracts a chunk of ice and sets it on a metal stand over the chalice. He turns to the gathered and raises his hands.

"The world will end in ice and fire!"

"The world will end in ice and fire," everyone except Eddy repeats.

Mr. Timberson takes a blowtorch from under the table, ignites it, and sets it up pointed at the ice. It begins to melt rapidly.

"We undertake the ritual to remind Yggdrasil of its promise, a promise stronger than gods. A promise of salvation for all who are cast out." He walks to the center of the formation and begins addressing individuals.

"Randly Silvester Timberson, Elder Father! Perched on the top point of Yggdrasil, you are the Hawk, the truth of wisdom, sheltered in the branches."

Dead Timberson makes no response.

"Eustace Silvester Timberson, Uncle and the Second Father! To the right of Yggdrasil in the raised position, you are the First Deer, the rains that shall come, sheltered in the branches."

"Sheltered in his branches," Father Eustace says.

"Lin Eustace Timberson, Daughter and the Mother of Silvius! To the right of Yggdrasil in the lowered position, you are the Third Deer, the winds that shall drive the storms, sheltered in the branches."

"Sheltered in his branches," Lin says.

"Elwood Eustace Timberson, Son and the Father of Silvius! To the left of Yggdrasil in the raised position, you are the Second Deer, the clouds that will cover the sky, sheltered in the branches."

"Sheltered in his branches," Elwood says.

"Anton Bosco, Adopted Son and Blood Brother to Elwood! To the left of Yggdrasil in the lowered position, you are the Fourth Deer, the groundwaters that will swell, sheltered in the branches."

"Sheltered in his branches," Anton says.

The ice slips from the stand and *klunks* into the wooden chalice. Mr. Timberson turns off the blowtorch and takes up the chalice, returning to his position.

"I, Miles Randly Timberson, High Father! Within the top of Yggdrasil, I am the Eagle, the speaker for Yggdrasil and leader of his cause, sheltered in the branches. I am sheltered in his branches."

He drinks once from the chalice and turns to dead Timberson, pouring a small trickle out over his shriveled lips. Mr. Timberson proceeds around the outside of the group, allowing each of the participants in the positions of Deer drink. He comes to Foster next.

"Foster Miles Timberson, Son and Brother and Heir. At the base of Yggdrasil, you are the squirrel Ratatoskr, scurrying massager and provoker of words, sheltered in the branches."

"I am sheltered in the branches." Foster takes a drink.

"Last, Eddy, the Caller of Yggdrasil." Mr. Timberson approaches her slowly. "You have no position on the tree. You are the final piece to an incomplete circle. Your place is as acting force instead of witness. The end of time requires agency." He holds the chalice out to her.

Eddy doesn't move; she just stares at him.

"Drink, child. Or else." He lifts it closer to her.

"Okay." She takes a small sip.

"Good."

Mr. Timberson returns the chalice to the table and takes up the mallet and a long iron spike. "Now! With Yggdrasil as witness, Deer and Hawk and Eagle as witnesses, Ratatoskr as witness, a token of the end shall be performed. A token as a reminder."

Mr. Timberson walks down the center of the tree trunk past Foster and to the wooden box within the roots. "Here! This one within the roots, twisting and gnawing." He gives the lid of a box a few taps with the mallet, then lifts the cover. For several seconds he stays crouched over the open box. Then he poises the spike and swings the mallet down. A loud hiss comes from the box, and Mr. Timberson strikes the spike several more times, driving it into the ground. He unfastens the sides of the box and reveals a snake pinned through its tail on the floor. "This snake is Nidhogg, enemy of Yggdrasil and the gods, gnawer of roots." Mr. Timberson returns to Eddy, holding out the mallet. "Take up the hammer, Caller of Yggdrasil, and destroy it."

"What? I—I can't do that."

"Child, this is your purpose. *Take* the hammer, and strike *down* Nidhogg."

"No."

He lowers the mallet. "And why do you refuse?"

Eddy looks at the snake. It's still hissing and has coiled itself around the piercing spike that's holding it steady. "It—it hasn't done anything. There's no reason. I can't."

"Ha. Whereas your compassion might be admirable in other circumstances, this is not the place, child. The next world will care about your compassion, not this one. This world only cares about your bravery. Strike it low!" He shoves the mallet against Eddy's chest.

"No!" Eddy takes the mallet and throws it aside. Several in the congregation gasp. "That too! You keep talking about another world and how you want this one to end. I'm not here for that. I'm here for that monster!"

"Oh how your perceptions are twisted, child." Mr. Timberson draws himself up to stand at his full height, hands clasped behind his back. "This ritual may not end the world outright, but it shall certainly hasten it along! It shall remind all creation and the gods themselves of what has been foretold, what is already transcribed as fact. That 'monster,' as you call it, is your only salvation from the freezing fires that shall wash over the land. You had only one chance today, and you have failed it."

Mr. Timberson beckons to the others, and they converge upon Eddy, taking hold of her arms and forcing her down to her knees.

"No! Let me go!" Eddy struggles but can't possibly overpower so many holding her. Foster remains to the sidelines, standing near the baby carriage and staring at the ground with his arms crossed.

Mr. Timberson retrieves the mallet and uses it to lift up Eddy's chin. "We shall try again another day, once the gravity of the ritual has been impressed upon you. But in the meantime, as my father always said, 'every maze must have its…consequences.' " He strides over to the snake and crushes its skull under the force of the wooden tool.

crush crush
buried under feldspar, down
so far under felds par all
the way to the core and
immobaile under so much weight

down, and chipped away slowly
pressssing
by underground rivers raging
benethe, under the crust,

mine. drowned by lungs filled
surface
with mud and you.

YOU ARENT READY FOR THIS

Splinter 26

Back at the house, Eddy is dragged upstairs, through the cluttered hallways, and into a study. Two of the four walls are lined with books, the third has a fireplace set into it, and the fourth holds the door through which they enter. Lin shoves the cushioned large-backed chair and its small table with burn marks on its surface to the side of the room. Verdi and Anton bring in two saw trestles on which they lay a large wooden board. Mr. Timberson steps forward.

"Now child, for your insolence you shall be justly punished. There is only one sentence within this family, and that is the board." He points to it with one slender finger. "Prepare him on it. Foster, fetch the pail and water."

Foster leaves as Eustace and Elwood start pulling off Eddy's shirt.

"No! No, stop!" Eddy grips the fabric as the whole thing gets bunched up under her arms, pinning one elbow awkwardly against her chest.

No one replies. The shirt is forced up farther, over her face, and someone pries her fingers one by one to unball her fist. Eddy strikes out with a foot and connects with someone's leg, and they grunt and recoil.

"Grab his legs!"

The shirt is pulled free, and she is lifted up to the board. Eddy tries to cover her chest, but her arms are pulled down to her sides as Anton starts wrapping duct tape around and around her ankles. Elwood is also binding up one wrist to a trestle leg, Eustace the other, and then they begin coiling the duct tape in opposite directions around her waist and stomach.

Eddy shakes her head back and forth, wiggling her whole body to fight free, but there is too much tape. Anton finishes and starts running tape over and around her shoulders. Soon she can hardly move at all. Eddy's head hangs off the board, and she sees the world upside down with blood running to her head as Foster returns with a metal bucket that is wider than it is tall. He sets it on the floor under Eddy's head. Everyone backs up near a wall, except Mr. Timberson, who remains near the board.

"All is prepared, child," Mr. Timberson says. "This is to be a lesson, and this is a place of learning. We are surrounded by elder books and tomes, teachings and stories with more wisdom in them than what the modern age can offer." He takes Eddy's head and turns it toward a bookcase. "You see those, child? Each one is worth more than the entirety of your life."

"Then why are you even bothering with me if I'm so worthless?"

"Because you are the Caller of Yggdrasil."

"No, I'm not! That's not me! I would kill him if I got the chance!"

"Fool. You can't kill something so cosmic. You simply do not understand yet, but that lack of understanding is understandable." Mr. Timberson smirks a moment. "You see, it is told that the Caller of Yggdrasil shall be an outsider chosen by Yggdrasil himself. Yggdrasil has revealed its avatar to you, therefore you must be the Caller of Yggdrasil. The fact you must come from without is indeed unfortunate. It means you have none of the proper discipline. But that is what this punishment shall help teach."

"I won't. I'll never do your ritual. I won't help the world end!"

"So you say now, and perhaps you truly will not. Only time shall tell. Pity you aren't female. Then we could have used you for something tangible, at least. Foster has my blood in him, my blood and my mother's blood, so he has the divine affliction within him even if he is too weak to display it. But as a person to whom Yggdrasil has revealed himself, you certainly would enable it. Truly, I am surprised you don't have Marfan syndrome yourself. Has anyone in your family? Your father or grandfather perhaps?"

"Fuck you." Eddy spits but misses Mr. Timberson.

"Ah. Finished talking, are you? Then we shall begin. But fear not, your punishment will only be in proportion to your misdeeds." He ties a blindfold over her eyes.

Nothing happens at first. A bit of water sloshes beneath Eddy's head, as if a cloth is being dunked and then rung out inside the bucket. This happens four times, and Eddy is shaking now. There is no other sound in the room besides the groaning from the pipes in the attic filtering down through the ceiling.

"These waters shall cleanse," Mr. Timberson says softly. "This act is done in accordance with our customs."

A few sprinkles of water drip down onto Eddy's face. "W-what are you—?"

Cold water covers her face. More than that, it's a drenched towel covering her face. Eddy tries to suck in air through the moisture but gets little more than a parody of a breath. She tries to shake her head, but two sets of hands are now keeping her face straight up.

It goes too long, her whole body squirming in the knots of duct tape. The cloth is raised, and Eddy gasps and coughs.

"Can't—can't breathe," Eddy spits out.

"I know," Mr. Timberson says. "And that was only a taste."

The cloth comes back down not as wet, but before Eddy was ready. She hasn't gotten a proper breath; she won't survive this. She sucks at the towel, some air coming through as it makes an O inside her lips. The water splashes beneath her and a small stream of icy liquid washes over her face through the cloth. Eddy gags, can't cough, shakes her whole body. Everything is dark and cold, and she cannot breathe, cannot get a single gasp.

The cloth is lifted, and Eddy is given only a few seconds to cough and spit out water. She gets two good breaths, and the cloth comes down again. More water. It flows into her nose. Makes her snort. As if it can help. She tries to spit, but the cloth simply catches the water and forces it back into her mouth. There is nowhere for the water to go except into her, pooling at the back of her mouth and draining the wrong way through her nose. Eddy thrashes her head, gaining a small movement, dislodging the cloth for but a moment, a half gasp, and it is righted.

"And I was just about to lift it, child. Must keep it a bit longer now."

Another stream of water drenches the cloth, and Eddy's back arches. The water gurgles in her mouth, and a second stream is poured over her as soon as the first is finished. Eddy thinks she is tearing up but can't tell since her whole head is soaked with cold water. She's shaking now, hands clenching and unclenching at random, white dots popping in her black vision.

The cloth is lifted halfway, not fully removed, and Eddy still can't rightly breathe past the coughing and the water in her throat. She turns her head, water dribbling over her cheek and through the stubble she has not been given the means to shave.

"Ple—ple—ple—" Eddy sputters.

"No."

The cloth is brought down again.

I'm gonna die. I'm gonna drown to death on a board in a mansion of crazies. Eddy doesn't have the strength to struggle now. The best she can muster is a small shaking of her head, but no more. She holds her breath and holds her breath and holds it and holds it until it feels that her lungs could rip open her chest and save her from this torment in a fatal explosion, but no. She gasps under the cloth and gets nothing but water as it streams over her, into her. Filling her up and surrounding her like rosca de reyes batter. She will be tucked away and lost in the baked cake until found sliced through and lodged as plastic in someone else's throat, hands grasping at her through flesh; with no time to help, the final obituary notice will be so underwritten it will make everyone cry all over again: poor, poor man to be done in by a fruitcake doll!

The cloth is lifted, and Eddy doesn't realize it at first until a hand slaps her across the face, and she gasps so loud and so wide they might think she is already a ghoul, unneeding of air but unable to relinquish it. For a near half minute Eddy thinks of nothing, merely breathing.

"Has he had enough?" the older voice rasps.

Silence.

"I think so," the youngest voice says.

"Be quiet. I decide."

The cloth comes down again. More water. Eddy is so cold and growing numb and thoughts empty, empty, empty, swallowed up by the endless ocean just beneath her scalp that keeps reaching up to take her head and body and pull her down into itself fathoms deep with kelp tendrils around each limb and whole body. Her head goes limp.

She wakes up—still on the board strapped down—being fanned, head held up. Shaking, whole face white and blue.

"Your punishment is over, child," Mr. Timberson says. "Let it be a fast reminder of your wrongdoing and what will come to you in the future if you continue to disobey."

Eddy just stares at the ceiling, eyes unfocused. Someone cuts the tape over her shoulders, and she is sat up, small rivulets of water slipping over her shoulders and chest.

"Take him to his room."

Hours later Eddy is still disoriented, her sleep fitful. She keeps waking in starts, thinking she can't breathe, but after sitting up and gasping at the air, she is struck by a wave of fatigue again.

The sun sets, and soon her room is too dark to be of any comfort at all. She huddles against the headboard under the blankets with her knees at her chest, staring at the door, listening to the hiss and gurgle and occasional knocking above her. Eddy thinks she might do anything to avoid the board again.

She wonders how many times Philip has tried to call her, wonders if he's tried to call at all. What if Adrastos's biological grandmother has called to see how the move from her house to the apartment is working out? What if Eddy's father has called? She probably doesn't need to worry about that happening, but what if?

A key clicks in the door lock, and Eddy is jolted from her thoughts. She scrambles off the bed and crawls underneath it.

The door only opens partway, stopping just before the hinges begin to squeak. A single set of feet tread lightly upon the floor.

"I know where you are," he says softly, then gets down on his hands and knees. It's Foster. "Sheets are a dead giveaway, strewn over like that. You need to make sure they stay on top of the bed."

"What do you want? Get away from me!"

"Calm down, will you? I'm letting you out."

"W-what? Really?"

"Yeah."

"Why?"

"Because you've seen him now." He stands back up and says something else Eddy can't make out.

Eddy slides out from underneath and gets to one knee on the opposite side of the bed. "What'd you say?"

Foster drops a skeleton key on the bed. "That goes to a few different doors. I'm gonna try to run. Don't follow me." He turns to leave.

"Wait. What did you say?"

Foster just stands in the doorway as if caught between two wires. "I said…if you hate him even half as much as I do…you'll kill him."

"What? Kill him? No. I can't kill someone."

"I think you will."

"Why don't you?"

Foster shakes his head. "I already tried, but then you showed up instead." He steps out into the hallway, leaving the door open.

Eddy stares at the doorway, then snatches up the skeleton key and peeks around the doorframe. The hallway is empty. And she is free.

woudl you promis never?
            promis never?

if my blood, blood is blasted
or/if, blood is plastered,
    drowned.
if blood like tears, if blood
in roots and viens and ckustters
wont be seen, spewed, hidden down
to stair or elevator or lift
or rope or ladder or step or wing
or STARR
        here. me.

would you? never? fulfill it?

would you?   would

                you

                MØNSTER

Splinter 27

The floorboards creak as Eddy sneaks down the hallway, and she freezes. She waits but doesn't hear anything. Is everyone else in bed? Eddy isn't sure how late it is.

She creeps along more slowly now, testing her steps before putting down her full weight.

Narrow points in the hallway created by the massive amounts of clutter make the effort more difficult. There are places where the passage between boxes or unused furniture becomes too thin to allow her to step somewhere without a creaky board. Eddy takes these steps as slowly as she can.

All she has to do now is get through tonight. Just get out of this house and get away from this crazy family, and she will be fine. She knows it.

The study is coming up, just the very next door on the left. Eddy slows to a halt several feet away. If Mr. Timberson is in there…well, he definitely deserves it. After what he did to her, after what happened to Adrastos, after everything. After all this and she hasn't even seen that monster in days. That Yggdrasil. The only monster she's seen has been Timberson.

Eddy presses up against the wall and peeks around the open doorway with one eye. A fire is crackling in the stone hearth with a large-backed chair pulled up to it. A puff of smoke coils up and drifts from the reclined figure: Timberson's leg is crossed over the other, a pair of faded slippers on his feet. He can't see her. She has the total element of surprise.

Oh, but she could do better than that. The pipes in the ceiling, the whole waterworks remade in the attic. She could destroy everything in that study, not just Timberson. Eddy sneaks past the open door, searching for stairs.

The first stairs she comes across lead down and out of the house. At the top she looks down, and for a moment Eddy knows she could just leave instead. But she turns away, not willing to just let this go. A growing urge inside is telling her she must do something.

She continues on and peeks through keyholes and open doorways, but the rooms are all bedrooms or storage rooms. One is totally empty. Eddy is nearing the end of the hallway, and she begins to worry that the way into the attic will be in a closet somewhere. That will mean backtracking and more time and less stealth. She isn't sure if she can get away with this crazy idea of water destroying the house.

The last door proves her better. Through the keyhole, Eddy can just make out a set of stairs in the gloom. The door is locked, but the skeleton key opens it. Eddy leaves the key in the hole and ascends into darkness.

A small circular window gives only the faintest of starlight from outside, and Eddy trips over something long and metal before even taking two steps. On her hands and knees she turns around, feeling the floor, and lays hands on a pipe wrench. She feels the whole thing to be sure and takes it up. It's heavier than Eddy expects, and cold.

Eddy stands back up and shuffles forward slowly, reaching her hand above her head to find a cord for a light. Soon she does find one, and the light reveals pipes on pipes, twisting about through the whole attic: the floor is knotted with copper tubing and connectors, and the walls are lined with white plastic pipes that jut off into the air at random intervals, ropes tied around pipes tied to the ceiling to suspend them, a rectangular desk sawed in half to lift one set of pipes near the stairs and another cluster against the far wall. No one except a contortionist could move farther into the attic than the small open space at the top of the stairs.

Eddy's heart quickens as the gurgling and hissing and whooshing of water through these tubes surrounds her as if the mansion itself had bowels. There are so many tubes that most of the walls are left in darkness because the piping blocks all light from the small bulb.

Eddy tightens her grip on the wrench in her hands. It's fifteen inches and blue, as if ready to ice over. She raises it above her head, targeting the nearest plastic pipe, and holds steady. She is preparing herself. She will strike the pipe and keep hitting it until it breaks and water gushes forth to run between wooden planks and plaster, trickling into every nook and cranny until the mansion itself is submerged—drowns—and the water bursts forth from the windows and doors, knocking them off hinges and sliding tracks.

That is what she will do. Eddy is ready. Eddy knows she is ready. But she can't. Her face screws up, and she clenches her teeth. *Not now. Please, please, not again.* The wrench will not come down. Her arms are locked over her head, and she keeps readying herself, not wanting to move just yet. Not just yet.

The shadows in the attic seem darker, and she knows this place has to go. Has to be destroyed. She has to do something. So move! This place is so empty, everywhere she's gone this past month, just emptiness and loss. The only thing in the world she has left is a hollow hole in her heart. And it clicks.

The heft of the wrench in her hands, the cold air consuming her, the creaky floorboards beneath her: it's all she has now. This single moment…and this emptiness. This here that isn't around her but within.

Eddy screams and smashes the wrench down, splintering through the pipe in one swing, and water blasts out and becomes a constant stream. She is soaked, but she doesn't care. Eddy screams again—eyes shut tight—as she keeps swinging, lashing out at the pipes around her, forcing anything out she can.

She breaks another and another, and soon Eddy is in the middle of the attic standing in a river of water that covers the entire floor, the house voiding out its innards even as she only rips the hole larger.

With heaving breaths, Eddy rests the wrench against her shoulder and walks back to the stairs, not wanting to check if she feels any different, listening to the muffled voices beneath her. She smiles slightly and catches her breath before returning to the second-floor hallway.

It's raining indoors. Water is dripping through the ceiling all over at a constant rate, small rivulets pouring out down the walls. The cardboard boxes are turning darker brown, and the water can't seep through the floorboards fast enough to prevent puddles from forming. A few voices are yelling downstairs. Mr. Timberson is yelling just a dozen feet down the hallway, in his study.

She could still leave. Instead she goes back to the study.

Eddy stands in the doorway, watching him run about the room collecting books and stacking them within his arms. He drops a pile on the desk and rips out a drawer, throwing its contents to the floor. He sets the drawer upside-down on top of the pile. Mr. Timberson makes for the bookcase again but notices Eddy and lurches to a halt.

His eyes bulge. "You! You—you did this! You did this, didn't you!"

"Why do you think I have this?" Eddy asks softly, raising the wrench a few inches off her shoulder.

"By the gods! You will burn for this! This treachery! You—! You—! Nidhogg! You *are* Nidhogg!" Spittle flies from his lips, his fingers curling in on themselves.

"No. *Cría cuervos y te sacarán los ojos.*"

Eddy runs forward, wrench held high. Timberson yells and tries to retreat but slips on several pencils he had scattered on the floor and falls backward to the ground. Eddy brings the wrench down hard, cracking Timberson's shoulder, and he screams.

Eddy screams louder. "This is for trans people!" *Thunk.* "And the Romanians!" *Thunk.* "For systems!" *Crunch.* "For everyone you would have trampled!" *Thunk.* "And this! This is for Adrastos!" *Crack!*

With each blow Timberson tries to crawl away, tries to plead or shield his body but the third hit breaks his arm, and the last swing Eddy aims straight for his head. She strikes dead center on the top of Timberson's skull, and it cracks loudly, sickeningly. Timberson's eyes roll up, and it looks for a moment like he might puke, but he falls to his side and does not move again.

Eddy doesn't stop.

The water is in her eyes, and the world is a blur, and she is burning with rage, unable to feel the cold water raining on her. She keeps smashing the wrench into

Timberson's head, voiding out his void, his temple caving in, his eyes breaking out of their sockets. With a final crushing blow Timberson's head splits open like a spilled bucket of ice: shards of skull attached to skin with bits of hair scatter over the floor. Pink and red brain matter gush out like toothpaste along with a rush of crimson blood. The red flows around Eddy's feet. She drops the wrench and takes a few steps backward before falling to the ground.

She sits in the water soaking through her pants and wipes her eyes clear to see what she has done. Oddly, perhaps, Eddy doesn't feel anything. She can only look at the crumpled corpse a few seconds before looking away.

"Fuck you," she mutters as the water and blood swirl around her.

Now it's over. She's killed him; she's butchered that monster. Eddy pushes herself to her feet and wobbles back to the door. She leans on the frame, and her hand leaves a bloody mark where she touches the wood. It soon washes away as Eddy shuffles back down the hallway.

if
the
storm
does
not
follow
you.

Don't go in its path.

Splinter 28

The house is silent now. People had been yelling downstairs, but not anymore.

Eddy has to keep wiping water from her eyes as she trudges down the stairs to the ground floor in heavy socks and pants. She is shaking again, with a splitting headache starting right about at the same spot where her wrench had struck Timberson. Where is everyone else?

I should have brought the wrench. What will I do if I run into someone else? But Eddy doesn't go back to get it. She keeps going down, holding the railing as she walks over the thin waterfall covering the steps. Most of the lights are still on, but a few are flickering and a few more have gone out from the water seeping into them.

Downstairs is not quite as bad as upstairs. Water is still dripping from above and running down the walls, but not as much. That will soon change. The carpet is already soaked through.

Down the main hallway is a junction, one turn leading over to the front entryway. One of the double doors is open, and Eddy smiles. That's probably where Foster ran out. Probably where everyone ran out. Eddy is just about to leave too, but something catches her eye down the other hall.

Her head snaps over, confirming the sight. A phone. An older-model rotary phone, but a phone nonetheless. Eddy smiles a little wider and goes to it. It has a dial tone. *Yes, yes.* She rotates each number for Philip in sequence, watching the small disk click back into position each time. It rings and rings and rings.

An older female voice answers. "Hello, you've reached the Espenson residence. Sorry we're not home—"

Eddy hangs up and tries again.

"Hello, you've reached the Espenson residence—"

"No. No, no, no," Eddy whispers. "Please get the phone. Please." She hangs up and redials.

"Hello, you've—"

Eddy exhales through clenched teeth. She closes her eyes, hoping desperately that someone will pick up before the automated message finishes. No one does, and the voice-mail machine beeps on.

She waits just a moment longer, and starts. "Uh, hey…uh, this is Eddy. Um, this—this message is just for Philip, please, just—just let him only listen to it. Philip, I'm—I'm really sorry. I can't, even, begin to describe what's happened. I was thinking about you though. Every day. I *didn't* forsake you. I promise. I promise." Eddy stops, unsure of what else she can even say. She opens her eyes and sees a stream of water is flowing right by the phone jack. She gasps. "Sorry, sorry. I think this phone is about to go out. I…I'm coming home. Soon. I dunno. I don't even know where I am." The stream of water is snaking about, undulating side to side. "No matter what happens, even if they, arrest me," she says, her voice cracking, "I really did care about you. I wanted us to—"

There is a slight pop in her ear, and the water is flowing over the phone jack.

"Dammit! No!"

Eddy hits the receiver down with her other hand and lets it loose, but nothing happens. There's no dial tone or sound of any sort. She sniffs, wipes more water from her eyes, and turns back to the front door. The rain keeps falling, the carpet a mire now. Eddy looks up at those double doors and stops in midstep.

Something is there, right there in the hallway. The falling rain is hitting something, running sideways and down the air as if clinging to something like a suggested silhouette. And the carpet. A set of footprints pressed into the carpet. Footprints too big to be natural.

Eddy doubles over, coughing uncontrollably. She almost feels like she will throw up, but that part never comes. After half a minute she gains some composure and looks up. The footprints are closer.

"No!" she chokes out.

Eddy staggers backward, pressing against the wall, back of her hand against her mouth to stifle the coughs. She glances at the stairs and back, and she has to run. Run or die. She doesn't breathe or think, she just runs, footfalls slopping against the carpet and slipping once on the stairs. Eddy falls forward, breaking her fall with her hands, but she bites her tongue and tastes blood. She doesn't feel the pain; she keeps scrambling up, finally getting her feet running.

Upstairs is saturated now, at least a quarter inch of water covering the floor. Eddy stumbles on the last step and falls sideways into a stuffed wolf, knocking clothing and hats across the floor before her. She tramples over them.

The house is much darker now; many of the lights have been blown out. Running down the hallway, past the study, Eddy almost falls as she abruptly stops herself by grabbing the door frame. Timberson is gone: his whole body disappeared from the place where Eddy had left him. Not even chunks of brain or skull fragments litter the ground. Even the blood is gone.

Eddy's breath is still caught up in her throat, and she can't scream or yell or say anything. Her legs shake and almost give out as she clutches the doorframe. Glancing back down the hallway from where she came, Eddy doesn't see anything, but she doesn't trust her eyes. With concentrated effort she forces her feet forward again, forces herself to keep running away from that thing.

The rain is much heavier here, and Eddy constantly has to wipe water from her face. She rushes past all the doorways blindly, not even thinking of where she's going. There has to be another set of stairs in a house this big.

If there is, she doesn't find them. The hallway ends in a window, right next to the door leading up into the attic. Eddy tugs on the handle, fingers slipping over water, but the door will not budge. It's locked again, and the skeleton key is gone.

Eddy chokes out a half sound like a *no* and pounds her fists on the wooden door. The wrench! Why hadn't she brought the wrench! She heaves in a deep breath, crying now, and pulls on the door once more. Eddy jerks her head to look back down the hallway, water droplets flying from her hair, and a set of footprints are displacing the flowing water on the floor.

She yelps and jumps away, the window sill hitting the small of her back. Eddy doubles over a moment as she turns around, gritting her teeth, and frantically tugs at the window, trying to pull it up, breaking a fingernail in the process.

"Ay! *Ugh.* No. Please, *no.*" Eddy leans again the sill, finger bleeding, staring out into the night, breath fogging up the glass. Her faint reflection looks back at her, tormented as she, but nothing else appears in the glass. Eddy closes her eyes and turns around.

For what feels like eight minutes, she just stands there, not looking. But it isn't that long. She opens her eyes, and the displaced water footprints are right in front of her. Eddy sniffs and swallows, wiping *the* water from her eyes one last time.

"I never deserved this," Eddy says, voice breaking. "Never."

Something unseen presses against her eyes, and the world goes black.

Time has passed in measures vague: leaves maturing, listless winds, all now falling from a branch. Nothing marked between these things. Not a thing connecting those dots of recognition here. Eddy wayward lost in sites similar, but not the same. There is grass around her toes, foreign grass like none she knows. Nothing like the grass from home. Eddy knows she wears a smock, white with red from dribbled paint running down as river streaks. Eddy's body, too, is changed: torso breasted like believed.

World has lost solidity. Any object she may touch tingles disagreeably. Walls and doors unopened here burn against uncovered skin. Inside buildings or in woods, not a source of light abounds; still though Eddy can perceive. One unknown and fuzzy man sits and works upon a desk—

jumbled figure quite unclear, hardly more than silhouette. Furthermore, her eyes now blur overlaid with glowing hue: vibrant blue around her sight.

Eddy passes through unseen.

Eddy drifts in random spots, places rarely picked by her. Shadow people all surround, every faded one is blurred, similar and indistinct. Height remains defined and seen, movements too are clearly made. Many taller, many walk. Eddy stands on concrete paths, shadows all maneuver past, not one even touching her.

Eddy passes through unseen.

Eddy never wearies here, neither pangs with hunger here. Something stronger gnaws on her, endless on her oblong heart: swelling up an urgent need, need to vanish from this place. Eddy stalks a shadow now: lacking any hard known facts clarifying who or what person Eddy follows here. She imagines him a man, owning perfect lips and black facial hair. A countenance Eddy cannot even see. Sight is lacking, but this one person feels like something she could have known: a back-pass link bridging phantom future-tense pathways she once fantasized, bred from youth's naïveté.

Glass upon a wall, and she shows no double image there. Eddy hears no person, can't even read emotions 'graved over any face: she can't puzzle through the spoken words curving over absent lips.

Eddy's body never moves; places simply change. A room filled with little cubicles—single light bulb dim in dark. Standing overlaid her picked person; they remain in one singular location. Thoughts trickle over, feelings drain into Eddy: shadow sight, taste, and smell a thousand times distant. Hardly greater than merely spark, or drop, or wisp.

These are not enough for her. Never satisfactory. Eddy grabs without avail. Fading fast and hollowed out. Gone and empty save this great, devouring homesickness.

Jacob H. Ramm

is very pleased to bring you this story, and hopes it doesn't exactly please you (if you know what he means). Ramm still believes we really need to get into space, but he would like to also point out that mirrors are kind of bothersome. He's currently working on the next book in the *Slender Cycle.*

Caterina Böhm

is a fantasy artist from Germany who works mostly with digital media. You can find her at grimae.deviantart.com.